SEVENS

WEEK 1:
SHATTERED

Scott Wallens

PUFFIN BOOKS

All quoted materials in this work were created by the author.
Any resemblance to existing works is accidental.

Shattered

Puffin Books
Published by the Penguin Group
Penguin Putnam Books for Young Readers,
345 Hudson Street, New York, New York 10014, U.S.A.
Penguin Books Ltd, 80 Strand, London WC2R 0RL, England
Penguin Books Australia Ltd, Ringwood, Victoria, Australia
Penguin Books Canada Ltd, 10 Alcorn Avenue, Toronto, Ontario, Canada M4V 3B2
Penguin Books (N.Z.) Ltd, 182-190 Wairau Road, Auckland 10, New Zealand

Penguin Books Ltd, Registered Offices: Harmondsworth, Middlesex, England

Published by Puffin Books,
a division of Penguin Putnam Books for Young Readers, 2002

1 3 5 7 9 10 8 6 4 2

Front cover photography copyright © 2001 Stewart Cohen/Stone
Back cover photography copyright (top to bottom) Stewart Cohen/Stone,
David Roth/Stone, David Rinella, Steve Belkowitz/FPG, Karan Kapoor/Stone,
David Lees/FPG, Mary-Arthur Johnson/FPG

Produced by 17th Street Productions,
an Alloy Online, Inc. company
151 West 26th Street
New York, NY 10001

17th Street Productions and associated logos
are trademarks and/or registered trademarks of Alloy Online, Inc.

ISBN 0-14-230098-5

Printed in the United States of America

PROLOGUE
PETER DAVIS, 1:20 A.M.

I'm somewhere I've been many times; I can feel it. Nothing looks familiar—everything's fuzzy, and the details keep changing. But the feeling I have in here, in this room—I've felt it before.

And then it comes to me, so obvious. I'm in my basement. I have to be. But it doesn't make sense—I don't see the Ping-Pong table or the NordicTrack anywhere. Still, I've been here enough times to recognize my basement when I see it, smell it, feel it. Suffocate in it. I hate it down here.

I glance down at the floor, and sure enough, there it is: that dirty-looking, gray carpeting with flecks of blues, reds, purples, greens, and browns scattered throughout. When I was little, I used to love this carpeting. I thought it looked like a whole bunch of the marbles I kept in Maxwell House cans in my closet squished together and flattened out. But now the colors seem to swirl, rush at me, contracting and expanding, making me dizzy. Making me nauseous.

It's freezing, of course. It always is. I'm cold, even in this stupid blue sweater vest that my mom made me wear for the occasion, and the light brown skin on my arms prickles with

1

goose bumps. Crap. Here it comes. I'm starting to get that uneasy feeling in the pit of my stomach. It's not the nausea, but the tightness. That feeling that makes me drip with sweat even though it's probably thirty degrees down here. My heartbeat picks up and my mouth dries out in anticipation.

There it is. I smell it with a sudden, sickening jolt. The air down here has been poisoned with a metallic scent. It smells putrid. Acidic. It reeks of death. Decay.

Fear—not the adrenaline-producing kind I used to feel when I'd race on my dirt bike or book from a store after having just swiped a pack of smokes, but the pure, unadulterated lose-your-breath, lose-your-stomach, lose-your-mind kind, the type I felt right before those blinding headlights crashed into my door, that brand of fear—bubbles straight up through my insides, travels through my veins, and cuts off my circulation. My brain is void of thoughts, void of feeling. There is only this all-encompassing panic. My heart is practically ricocheting against my chest, but I don't move. I'm trapped in this damn wheelchair, but even if I could get somewhere, what's the point? Why leave? Why not just wait for it to come and claim me and end my misery now?

Sweat is running out of my pores, my stomach feels tensed and hollowed out at the same time, and I'm shaking like a five-year-old. Still, I'd rather sit it out and wait than try to make it out of here. Rather just ride out the fear and get this whole thing over with. I've been waiting for this my entire life.

Suddenly, as I stare upward, I see a door at the top of a very long staircase. The stairs seem to go much higher than they should, but I still recognize my basement door at the top. The door swings open, letting in a bright shaft of light from upstairs. I squint and curse under my breath, thinking someone has come to rescue me. But then my heart jumps, my shoulders tense up, and I see that is not the case. Not by a long shot. Kids, little kids, are falling down the stairs. Falling hard, as if they've been pushed. They cry and shout out as they tumble down the endless steps. I want to cry as well, I want to scream as I see these little kids hit the carpeting with such force. But I am too scared, too numbed by fear, to do either. All I can do is count the kids. One, two, three . . . six. There are six of them, crying and wailing, and now I just want to escape, get away from this.

The kids try to pull themselves up, but they can't seem to move. They squirm and they wiggle, but they don't budge. It's like they're glued to the floor. They can't get away.

And then they lift their faces.

I grip the ice-cold armrests on my wheelchair as I realize that I know these kids. Knew them, actually. Well, I still know them, but they should be my age. Right now they appear to be frozen in time. They look about ten years old. About the age when I did really know them. When we were all friends. When . . .

I feel like I'm choking, like I can't catch my breath. All six of them—Meena, Jeremy, Danny, Jane, Karyn, and Reed—gaze up at me with fear-filled childlike eyes. Then Meena begins to speak. Her voice sounds disjointed and eerie. A grown-up voice coming from a kid's mouth.

Peter. Help. Me.

Soon they all join in. Help, Peter. Peter. Help. Me. Help. They're all still squirming, trying to unglue themselves from the

3

floor, their voices becoming more and more insistent. Louder.

Their pleading chant invades my brain, causes a buzzing in my ears, a pounding behind my eyes. I can't take it. I want to yell at them to shut up, but I can't seem to open my mouth.

I clench my jaw in anger. What the hell are they talking about? They want me to help them? How do they think I'm going to pull that off? Don't they see that I'm stuck in a chair?

Then something shifts inside me. I'm overcome by a peaceful, calming feeling. It's a warmth that starts in my shoulders and slowly works its way over me, around me, through me. Something, not a voice, but something like a sixth sense, tells me to look down and I do. And there's no wheelchair. Just my legs. Standing. On their own.

I'm not paralyzed.

I bolt up in bed, waking with a start. Cold sweat dripping from my forehead, my first instinct is to look at my legs. I throw off my comforter and there they are. Those useless slabs of flesh, lying there like two pieces of meat. I could plunge a butcher knife into my calf and I wouldn't feel a thing. All because of a spinal injury. A blow to the back, and you never walk again.

I lie back on my sticky, drenched pillow, the images from the nightmare still fresh and vivid in my mind. I get angry at myself for mistaking the vision of me standing on my own two legs as reality for even one half-asleep second.

I close my eyes and I can still hear Meena, Karyn, Danny, Reed, Jane, and Jeremy chanting. *Help.* I can still see their pathetic ten-year-old faces peering up at me. I scoff at my own idiocy. As if those people would ask me to help them. As if I could.

It was all just a nightmare. Nothing but a dream.

CHAPTER ONE

"Meena, sweetie, I just don't understand why you need to go out when it's already so late," Meena Miller's mother says as they stand together in the foyer, waiting by the window for Meena's ride. Meena's getaway car. "You've been baby-sitting all day, and you won't have your own car in case you're having a bad time and you want to leave." She reaches out with both slim hands and tucks Meena's long dark hair behind her ears.

"Mom, please," Meena says, swatting her mother's arms away. Her heart is pounding spastically in her ears and all the muscles in her body seem to be coiled with nervous tension. The last thing she wants is to be touched. She reaches up and pulls her hair out again, letting it fall over her face the way she likes it. "God, can't I even do my own hair?"

Meena watches her mother's face. The scrutiny in her light brown eyes as she pulls her hands away. The smooth, white skin such a different color from her own. The creases around her mouth that grow deeper whenever she speaks to Meena about parties, drugs, boys, grades.

Her mother has been looking at her that way ever since

Meena can remember. Probably ever since the adoption agent handed an infant Meena over to her and her husband seventeen years ago. Her parents must have gazed down at the tiny Vietnamese eyes, the dimpled brown skin, the tufts of black hair and thought, *You need us. We will protect you.*

Sometimes Meena has the feeling her parents look at her and still see that baby.

"And it's not that late," Meena adds, glancing out the window, hoping to see the one headlight that still works on her friend Dana Kreiss's car. She glances at her watch. "It's only five after nine."

Then she notices her hand is shaking, and she shoves it into the front pocket of her jeans. She has to get out of here. If she doesn't get out of here and expend some of this pent-up energy soon, she is going to come right out of her skin.

"Well, I want you home by twelve," her mother says, turning to head back into the kitchen.

"Are you kidding?" Meena blurts out. Her mother freezes and slowly turns again, arching one eyebrow at the outburst. "It's Saturday night!" Meena presses, ignoring the familiar telltale signal in her mother's expression. Knowing she'll get nowhere. "Noah and Micah didn't even *have* a curfew when they were seniors."

"And you are not your brothers," her mother says. Then, as if that is a sufficient argument to end any conversation, she turns again and disappears into the brightly lit kitchen.

Meena feels a sudden intense urge to scream.

As if she isn't well aware that she isn't her brothers. Not male and therefore not capable of standing on her own. Not white in an all-white family and therefore in need of special protections. Not related by blood to her parents and therefore requiring extra assurance. Extra love. Extra coddling.

Follow her, a little voice in Meena's mind shouts so loudly, she swears she can hear her ears ringing. *You're not a baby. They can't treat you like one anymore.* But she's rooted to the spot. Meena doesn't talk back to her mother and father. Never has. It's just not in her. And what happened tonight doesn't change a thing.

A small smile forms on Meena's lips, stretching the skin on her cheeks.

What happened tonight changes everything.

That kiss. That kiss. That kiss. It was unbelievable. It was surprising. It was like nothing she'd ever experienced before. Partially, of course, because Meena had never been kissed before tonight. But she is sure all kisses can't feel like this one did. This one was forbidden. It was mature. It was a grown-up kiss.

Meena Miller is not a baby anymore.

Still grinning, Meena bites her bottom lip and tears spring to her eyes.

Stop it, she tells herself. *This is not a good thing. You know it's not. I can't believe you're even smiling about this.*

Pushing the negative thoughts aside—the guilt that's been trying to gnaw at her every moment since it happened, the queasy little question of blame, of sin—Meena returns her attention to the window and actually jumps when Dana's car pulls onto her street.

"Bye!" Meena shouts as she rips open the door.

The gust of cold October air that hits her face along with the loud wail of the stereo screaming through the windows of Dana's car seems to blast away the dark thoughts and giddiness prevails. It's been ages since she's been to a party, and the noise, the dancing, the crush of people is exactly what she needs.

Just don't think about it, Meena tells herself. *Don't think about it, and everything will be fine.*

Meena slams the door and jogs across the lawn to Dana's waiting car.

• • •

Right at this moment, at nine-thirty on Saturday night, Jeremy Mandile couldn't have it any better. He knows this. He's certain of it. And everyone in his car seems to be feeling the same vibe.

After all, Jeremy is driving to a huge house party over at Luke Waller's house, which is bound to be a slammin' time. Tara Healy, Jeremy's gorgeous and sweet girlfriend, sits in the passenger seat next to him, laughing hysterically at something her friend Lainie Cruz, who's sitting in back, just said. The latest Everclear song comes on the car stereo, and Mike Chumsky, Lainie's boyfriend and Jeremy's fellow football team member, leans forward from his seat behind Jeremy and says, "Yo, turn it up. I love this tune."

Jeremy obliges, turning the dial on the radio as he makes a left turn. The catchy riff of the song pumps him up even more, makes him feel totally high on life. As the crisp autumn night air breezes in through his half-open window and hits his face, Jeremy thinks, *It really doesn't get much better than this.*

Jeremy glances over at Tara. She grins, and that crazy adorable dimple appears on her left cheek. Jeremy grabs her soft, delicate hand and kisses it.

"Oh, please. You guys are so cute, it's nauseating!" Lainie bellows from the back. Jeremy releases Tara's hand and they both laugh. They're used to friends complaining about what a perfect couple they are . . . and it doesn't bother them in the least.

The Everclear song peters out and Ed Ozone, the station's grating DJ, shouts enthusiastically about the thrill of mail-order teddy bears. Jeremy quickly turns the volume back down.

"You think anyone from Kennedy is going to be there tonight?" Lainie asks, referring to their rival high school.

Jeremy brakes at a stop sign, then turns back to glance at Lainie. Kennedy beat them in football a couple of weeks ago, and it's a bit of a sore subject among the Falls High team. "Why would they be?"

Lainie shrugs, her brown eyes widening. "I think Luke hangs with some of those guys."

"Oh, man," Mike complains, slumping into his seat. His stocky, stereotypical jock body dominates the back of

Jeremy's black Jetta. Mike points a finger at Lainie and Jeremy smiles, noticing that Mike's arm looks thicker than Lainie's leg. "I'll tell you what. If I see Dowager there, I am not holding back."

Jeremy gets a bad taste in his mouth at the mention of Sam Dowager, the Kennedy Tigers' linebacker. The idiot got into a fight with Reed Frasier after their game because of a brutal late hit that Dowager flattened Reed with in the fourth quarter.

Lainie pushes Mike's finger away from her face. "What're you telling me for? I didn't invite them."

"I think Sam Dowager would know better than to show up at a Falls party," Tara comments. She checks her reflection in the vanity mirror to make sure her short brown hair looks okay, but Jeremy doesn't know why she bothers. Her hair always looks perfect.

"Then again, the guy *is* a moron," Jeremy says with a short laugh.

"That's what I'm talking about, bro," Mike says, laughing appreciatively. "The dude deserves to be punished. *Obliterated*."

Jeremy rolls his eyes, smiling. At times, Mike's meathead factor can be rather amusing.

"Hey, hey, you know who *would* be funny to see, though?" Mike blurts out. Jeremy can feel Mike grabbing the back of his seat as he leans forward.

"This is going to be good," Lainie says sarcastically.

But Mike doesn't even seem to hear her. "Josh Strauss,"

10

he says. "You know, their fag mascot? Maybe he'll bring his little boyfriend."

Jeremy clenches the steering wheel, no longer amused. It's one thing to act like a meathead. But a brainless bigot?

"You know, you sound like an idiot when you say crap like that," Jeremy snaps.

"What? What did you just say?" Mike demands. Jeremy glances at Mike in the rearview mirror and sees that Mike's face is turning pink, as it always does when he's gearing up for an argument or a fight.

"He's right, you know," Lainie puts in, but Mike waves her off.

Jeremy lets out a frustrated sigh. Sometimes he seriously wonders why he's friends with Mike. "I know Josh, okay?" Jeremy says, irritated by the edge he can hear in his own voice. "I work with him at my parents' halfway house. He's cool." Jeremy focuses on the road ahead. "Gay or not."

Mike is silent for a moment—the entire car is silent—and Jeremy hopes that he's shut Mike up for a while. Then Mike says, "Oh . . . I get it." There's an annoying lilt to his tone.

Tara shoots Jeremy a sympathetic look. She knows as well as Jeremy does what a jerk Mike can be.

Lainie lets out an exaggerated groan. "Mike. Let it go."

But Mike doesn't acknowledge her comment. "What do you and little Joshie Strauss *do* at work together, J.?" Mike teases. Jeremy comes to a stop at a traffic light and he glances at Mike in the rearview mirror again. He sees that Mike's brown eyes are all lit up, like he's ready to go in for the kill.

11

"Are you getting it on with the queer boy?" Mike laughs. "Tara," he says, clicking his tongue with mock sympathy. "I hate to be the one to inform you that your boy here is gay." And with that, Mike starts to convulse with laughter at his own highly uncreative joke.

The light turns green and Jeremy slams on the gas, causing the car to bolt forward. His hands hurt from clenching the steering wheel so tightly. A million expletives run through his brain, but what can you actually say to such a complete ass?

Tara wastes no time in speaking up. "Please, Mike. Jeremy is about as gay as Brad Pitt, and you know it."

"Hey, I'm just putting some facts together, that's all," Mike responds. "Jeremy lo-oves Jo-*osh*, Jeremy lo-oves Jo-*osh!*" he singsongs happily.

"Really?" Tara twists around in her seat so that she's looking right at Mike. Jeremy has no doubt that she's giving him her patented don't-screw-with-me glare. "That's interesting. Because you're the one who seems to be overly interested in other guys' sexuality. In which case, the facts indicate that you're probably the one who swings the other way."

Lainie lets out a little laugh, but Mike is dead silent. Jeremy knows that Mike doesn't have the IQ necessary to muster up a comeback and he smiles to himself, glad that the jerk was properly put in his place. He reaches for Tara's hand and squeezes it, thankful that he has her by his side.

Tara shoots him a sly smile, obviously pleased with herself, and Jeremy chuckles. Then he turns the radio back up, loosens his grip on the wheel, and swings the car onto

12

Luke Waller's street. He checks in the rearview mirror again and can see that Mike is pouting like a little boy.

Jeremy runs a hand over his head, feeling his gelled, spiky dark hair. He lets out a deep breath. His perfect night was briefly interrupted by the reminder that he's got such an unenlightened friend. But tonight's all about fun, and Jeremy's sure they'll be back on track with that goal in no time.

• • •

Peter sits motionless, staring at the inside of the front door as his father reaches across it to turn the doorknob. His mother stands behind him, hands on the handles of his wheelchair, at the ready. It takes two people to get him out of the house. Him. Peter Davis. A person who used to leave his house at all times of night and day undetected and through any opening possible. Front door, back door, bedroom window. Now he can't even open the door—hasn't yet mastered the art of pulling it open and maneuvering his chair out of the way at the same time.

"Have fun tonight, son," his father says, sounding not unlike a radio announcer hawking laundry bleach. A little too enthusiastic.

"Uh . . . right," Peter says as his mother pushes him with a bang and a jolt over the threshold.

"Gotta get that fixed," she says with an embarrassed, girlish giggle. "Peter," she says to his father, the elder Peter. "Make a note to get that fixed, would you?"

Peter's father nods and moves away from the door, into the den, where all notes are written and then promptly forgotten. Peter's mom wheels him to the center of the porch, and Peter expects her to then follow his dad back inside. There's no reason for her to sit out here in the cold with him and wait for his friends to show. Unless, out of some sudden curiosity, she actually wants to see what they look like.

"Thanks, Mom," Peter says, glancing up at her. She just smiles awkwardly, standing there with her fingers laced together, the door to the house open, spewing out the heat that is—as always—turned up to Caribbean-like temperatures.

"Oh! You're okay?" she asks, prompted by some nonexistent comment from him. She pushes her light brown bangs out of her eyes, and her face pales. "I mean . . . are you going to be okay out here by yourself?"

Peter swallows back the bile that rises in his throat. His mother thinks everything she says is wrong. And even though half of it *is,* he can't take it. Can't take the fact that she's so nervous around him now. So uncertain and eager to please. It's a bit much to take when a little over a month ago—before the accident—she barely acknowledged his existence.

"I'm fine," he makes himself say. "I'll see you later."

"Okay," she says. She moves away, but slowly. "Have fun."

Peter doesn't breathe again until the door behind him closes.

He pulls his hands into his sleeves and waits. He's already freezing, but he doesn't care. It's about a quarter to ten on a chilly October night and his denim jacket is not enough to keep him warm. But he's not about to go back inside. No way. He's not going to go through it all again.

He sighs and watches the little cloud his breath makes float into the air and disappear. How did he get here? How did he get to a place where just leaving the house is a drama?

Peter is snapped out of his pathetic ruminations by the sound of screeching tires. He spots Keith Kleiner's black Land Rover turning the corner onto his street. As he watches the souped-up SUV near the curb in front of his house, he can't help but smile sarcastically. Peter hangs out with Keith more than anyone else in his crowd, but the guy is actually kind of a jerk. He's always acting like he has it so hard, like there's so much he needs to rebel against, while the truth is that Keith gets anything he wants. Peter knows that money doesn't solve your problems and that Keith's parents aren't exactly the most wonderful people in the world. But still, they throw him concert tickets, ski trips, every high-tech gadget they can find. Money sure doesn't hurt.

Keith pulls his car to a stop and Peter wheels himself down the ramp his parents had installed on the porch a few weeks ago. He hates the ramps. Every time he uses one, he remembers how he used to run up and down them as a kid— waiting for his mother to pick him up outside the library or in front of the school. Back then he'd never seen anyone use them. He'd thought they were there for his entertainment. Now they're just a constant reminder of what used to be.

"Yo, Davis," Max Kang says in his typically monotone way when he steps out of the passenger side of the car.

"Hey," Peter responds. Max isn't much to look at—a

15

fact he acknowledges himself with self-deprecating remarks whenever he gets the chance. His skin is covered with acne and his greasy dark hair hangs over his smallish eyes. Even so, Peter feels a rush of relief when he looks at him. Finally. Peter is going to have a normal Saturday night hanging with his friends. It's the first time since the accident just over a month ago and it's not a moment too soon.

Keith runs around the front of the car in his typically manic way. He reaches out to slap Peter five in greeting but hesitates slightly. Peter doesn't need to be a psychic to realize that the chair is weirding his friend out. He's glimpsed that flipped-out look in plenty of people's eyes recently, and even though Keith has seen Peter a number of times, he's obviously still not used to Peter being paralyzed.

Neither is Peter.

"So where's Doug?" Peter asks, referring to their friend Doug Anderson, who usually comes along on these ride arounds.

Keith shrugs.

"Something with his family," Max says vaguely.

"Come on, let's get going," Keith jumps in.

Peter nods, running a hand over his shaved head. "Yeah. Cool. Let's go."

Then something happens that Peter knows he would find funny if it happened to anyone else but him. Keith and Max both turn slightly, as if they're about to head back into the car and just leave Peter there, clearly forgetting that he can't exactly make it into the Land Rover on his own. Then they both seem to register it at the same time: they need to help Peter inside.

Max and Keith simply stand there stupidly for a moment, glancing from Peter to the SUV and back to Peter. It's like they can't figure out how to proceed. Peter knows he should clue them in, but the whole situation is so uncomfortable, he can barely speak. He feels his face heating up.

Keith fidgets with the black frames of his glasses, something he does whenever he's nervous or anxious. "So, uh, we gotta carry you in, right?"

"Yeah," Peter says, his eyes darting away from Keith's. This is the worst part. Peter can deal with awkwardness . . . sort of. But now he senses their pity. And that is something he cannot take.

"You get the right, I'll take the left side," Keith tells Max. For not the first time since the accident, Peter feels like an inanimate object. Something to be picked up and moved. Pushed around.

As Peter's two friends carry him over to the car, he has to crack a joke to break the weirdness of the moment. He needs to make them stop pitying him.

"You know, I had a nightmare about this last night," Peter says as Keith slowly lets go, allowing Max to ease him into the backseat. Max glances at Peter, one of his almond-shaped eyes visible through his shaggy hair.

"I mean, you two carrying me around. How scary is that?" Peter explains. He means it as a joke, but as it comes out of his mouth, it doesn't sound like one. He sounds strained. Forced. Max smiles slightly and Keith doesn't even respond.

Feeling more humiliated than before, Peter explains how to collapse his wheelchair so that they can stow it in back of the Land Rover. After what feels like an eternity, Keith and Max get in the car and Keith starts up the engine.

Peter hopes the weirdness will disappear, he prays their pity will evaporate, but that doesn't happen. Keith and Max are silent as they drive off, and they both seem to have a hard time looking back at Peter. Keith still fidgets with his damn glasses every couple of seconds and Max stares out the window so intently, you'd think the passing houses were showing him the meaning of life.

This pisses Peter off. He was looking forward to tonight. Looking forward to going out and finally feeling somewhat normal. Well, he's not going to let them ruin it. He's going to act like things are normal. As if they are the way they were before.

"C'mon, let's get this night started," Peter says, leaning forward and poking his head between their two seats. Thank God he can still move his torso. They both glance at Peter and he adds, "Who has the alcohol?"

Keith grins. "Now we're talking," he responds.

Max grabs a can of Coors from the paper bag between his feet and passes it back to Peter.

Peter takes the can in his hands and sits back as Max turns up the stereo. He regards the Coors for a moment, thinking about the drunk driver who relegated him to a wheelchair. Wonders what that guy had been drinking that night. Was it beer? Or was it something harder? Maybe it was a few cans just like this one that made him what he is today. Made him this useless thing that needs to be carried. Needs his ramps. Needs his parents. Took him from being a person who needed no one and turned him into a no one who needs help with everything.

Peter pops the can and takes a swig, closing his eyes.

The last time he was in a car with his friends, drinking, he had his legs taken away. Maybe the second time will be the charm. Maybe if Keith chugs some of the beer, too, he'll get them into an accident and Peter will die this time.

Peter lifts the can. Downs some more.

Cheers.

• • •

"It's my two favorite women!" Luke Waller shouts over the pounding music and the din of voices that come pouring out the front door of his house when he opens it. Meena takes one look at her friend's outfit and laughs. He's wearing a T-shirt with a fake tuxedo printed on it over a pair of Hawaiian shorts, his bony legs exposed in all their hairy whiteness.

"Aren't you freezing?" Meena asks, ducking inside, followed quickly by Dana.

Luke shakes a half-empty bottle of vodka in front of her face. "This'd keep a naked person warm at the North Pole," he says, holding the bottle out to her. "Wet your whistle?"

Meena, as always, reflexively lifts her hand and shakes her head. Luke knows she doesn't drink, but at parties he never

19

misses the chance to offer her alcohol. It's like he doesn't understand why anyone would ever want to be sober.

"I'll take some of that," Dana says, grabbing the bottle out of his hand and taking a long swig.

Meena wrinkles her nose and starts scanning the party for any signs of dancing. She still feels like her insides are shaking and she knows that if she can just let loose to some good, thumping dance music, she'll be able to lose herself. She'll be able to get out of her brain. And that's all she wants right now, even if it's just for a few minutes.

"Are you looking for *Justin?*" Dana teases, throwing her arm around Meena's neck and making a big show of looking around the room.

Meena's heart takes a nervous skip at the sound of Justin's name. Justin Wigetaw, the guy she's liked since freshman year and whom her friends endlessly needle her about. Funny, she hadn't even thought about Justin until right this moment. She'd spent hours before every other party she'd been to for the last three years obsessing over what Justin would think of her outfit and her hair and her makeup. Now, suddenly, it's like the whole, disgraceful, unrequited love scenario is wiped from existence. Is that all she needed to do to get over it? To find someone else?

Huh. Cool.

"No, I am not looking for Justin," Meena says with a smirk. "I am looking for a dance floor."

At that moment, as if whoever's in charge of music heard her mental plea, a retro Madonna tune, one of Meena's favorite songs to dance to, pounds through the house. Meena hears a quick round of female squeals of approval coming from the living room and knows some of her friends are in there dancing.

"I'll be back," she tells Dana and Luke. On her way to the living room she peels off her jacket and tosses it onto a chair with a pile of others. It's no surprise that the girls doing the dancing are none other than Jeannie Chang, Gemma Masters, and Karyn Aufiero, a troika of the beautiful people and, of course, members of the cheerleading squad.

Meena immediately joins them, moving to the beat of the music. Everyone yells their hellos, and Karyn's is fairly cold. Meena's heart drops at her friend's manner, but she's not all that surprised. Karyn's been weird around her ever since Meena missed her birthday party a couple of weeks ago. She'd told Karyn she needed to baby-sit, but that didn't seem to be a good enough excuse for the divine Miss Aufiero.

Meena ignores the slight and closes her eyes, reminding herself that the whole point of this night is to stop thinking. Besides, if Karyn wants to be mad at her, that's her problem.

You weren't really baby-sitting, though, the little voice in Meena's mind whispers. *Not all night, anyway. You were with* him, *remember? Remember the wine? Remember how sophisticated and special you felt? Remember how you were going to leave to make the end of Karyn's party, but he convinced you not to? Convinced you to stay with him?*

It's all Meena can do to keep from groaning aloud in

21

frustration. Why won't her subconscious just leave her alone for five minutes? She takes the dancing up a notch, climbing up onto the coffee table and kicking a few magazines onto the floor to make room for herself.

"Go, Meena!" Gemma yells out with a laugh.

Meena simply smiles in response, forcing herself to look like she's having fun. She closes her eyes, pushes her hands into her hair, and holds her head as she dances.

Just breathe, she tells herself, inhaling the scent of the sweet air freshener Luke's mom uses mixed with the tangy smell of spilled beer. *Keep moving and don't think.*

But it doesn't work. She starts feeling his lips again. Feeling his fingertips on her face. Hearing the throatiness of his voice as he tells her how much he cares for her. How beautiful and sweet she is.

Meena dances a little more slowly as the images take over her thoughts, the fake smile falling away from her face. But she should be happy, shouldn't she? After all, this is what she's always wanted. It's finally happened. The crush that she's had forever has finally turned into something more. She should be elated. Lovesick. Floating on air.

So why is it that all she wants to do is throw up?

Stepping shakily down from the table, Meena quickly bolts from the room, ignoring the stares and the shouts of her friends, calling after her, asking her what's wrong. All she can think about is the location of the nearest bathroom.

CHAPTER TWO

There's a line at the downstairs bathroom and as Meena's stomach rises up violently, she realizes the stairs are not an option. Instead she turns and rushes out the front door, hoping there won't be anyone she knows out there to witness what is undoubtedly going to be a very messy display.

But the second she takes one breath of the frigid fresh air, her stomach calms itself slightly. It's still turning, but she no longer feels like she's in immediate danger. Slowly Meena sits down on the little wrought iron bench on Luke's front step and bends at the waist, putting her head between her knees.

"Okay, feeling better," she whispers to herself. "Everything's fine. Everything's fine."

Then a hand lands on her back and Meena jumps up, startled nearly out of her skin.

"Sorry!" Justin Wigetaw takes a few steps back, arms raised in surrender, looking just as scared as Meena feels. "I just wanted to see if you were okay."

Meena's hand is over her heart as she struggles to catch

her breath, at the same time struggling to come to grips with the fact that Justin Wigetaw, *the* Justin Wigetaw, has come to check on her. That he is, in fact, standing there, his scruffy brown hair curling around his forehead, looking at her with a concerned expression on his WB-worthy face.

"I'm . . . I'm fine . . . thanks. Sorry I wigged out," Meena says, letting her hands drop. She laughs a nervous laugh. "But thanks for your concern."

Meena adds a self-deprecating smile and starts to sit down, but her legs are shaky and she ends up falling into the bench, hard. She manages to cover well and smiles up at Justin. Her heart is pounding just like it always does when he's within a five-yard radius, despite the fact that just minutes ago she thought he didn't matter anymore. Obviously he can still have an effect on her. Big time.

Then the unimaginable happens. Justin sits down next to her.

"It's no problem," he says, toying with the frayed hem of his blue-and-green flannel shirt. "I wanted to get out of there for a couple of minutes, anyway."

"Oh," Meena says. Great. *Oh.* Very articulate.

"You know, you were amazing in that swim meet last week," he tells her, turning in his seat to face her better. "I mean, you came out of nowhere."

Meena feels a burning blush wash over her face and looks down at her hands. "You were there?" she says, unable to believe that Justin would ever attend one of her swim meets. Only about five people ever showed up to watch. Meena never even bothers to look at the stands anymore. Except that day . . . that day someone else had come to watch her for the first time. It was no wonder she hadn't noticed Justin's presence.

"Yeah," Justin says. He clears his throat. Looks down at his fraying hem. Blushes a bit himself. "I don't, you know, usually go, but that day I was getting out of practice and I saw you waiting by the door in your suit and I thought, hey, school spirit and all that."

Meena's heart is going crazy at this point. Is Justin Wigetaw actually getting tongue-tied here? Is it even remotely conceivable that now, after all this time, after all the day-dreams, after all the unsent e-mails in which she confessed her love, after the pages upon pages of notebooks covered with M. M. + J. W. . . . now he has decided to . . . *like* her?

Meena glances at him and he seems to be waiting for an answer.

"That was cool of you," she says. "To stay for the meet."

And then it's happening. And it's happening just the way Meena has imagined it hundreds of times. Justin's clear brown eyes search her own, and then they move to her lips. There's a distinct sizzle of energy in the air between them and goose bumps pop out all over her arms. Before she can even register shock, his mouth is moving ever so slowly toward hers. His eyes are closing. Meena is about to have her second kiss. On the exact same night as she had her first.

And then the nausea is back.

"I have to go inside," she blurts out, standing so quickly, her elbow knocks into Justin's chin with a distinct crack.

Omigod, you're such an idiot. What are you doing? This is Justin Wigetaw!

She only has a split second to take in the expression of bewildered mortification on Justin's face before she flings open the front door to the house and loses herself in the crowd.

• • •

Jeremy is not much of a drinker, but he decides to head over to the keg to get another beer for the heck of it. That is, until Meena Miller comes tearing past him and Reed Frasier and runs up the stairs, looking white and clammy and altogether like she's about to lose her dinner. Suddenly another beer doesn't seem like the best idea to him.

"Man," Jeremy says to Reed as they both watch Meena's feet disappear up the stairs, "she is not looking too good."

Reed shakes his head, crossing his arms over his broad chest. "What's going on with her lately?"

"I don't know—it's not like she's a drinker," Jeremy says. "She probably got sick off of one beer." He quickly takes a step to the left, narrowly avoiding a near collision with a sophomore carrying one too many cups of beer. Accident averted, Jeremy steps over beside Reed again. "You think she's wasted?"

"Nah, I'm not talking about drinking," Reed says. He pulls off his worn-out Syracuse baseball cap, ruffles his thick red hair, then places the hat back on his head, pulling the rim down low so that Jeremy can barely see

Reed's bright blue eyes. "She's been completely antisocial ever since school started. She bailed on Karyn's birthday dinner—you know, when we all went to Theo's Grill a couple of weeks ago? She said she had to baby-sit or something."

"Well, maybe she did," Jeremy says with a shrug. "People do baby-sit, you know."

"Yeah, but she used the same excuse for the athletic dinner *and* the homecoming dance, and this is the first time I've seen her at a party in weeks," Reed explains. "She used to come to everything."

"So . . . what . . . you think she's not actually baby-sitting?" Jeremy says with a smirk. "That's a little paranoid, isn't it?"

"I don't know, but you'd think she could give up a few dollars to go to one of her best friends' birthday parties," Reed answers.

Jeremy laughs and shakes his head, leaning back against the wall. "Dude, don't you think you're a little biased in this situation? Karyn's like your best friend, so I'm guessing your information here is kind of one-sided."

"Yeah, true," Reed acknowledges with a one-shouldered shrug. "But Karyn *is* pretty upset about it. And she also says that she and her friends are starting to think that Meena has just decided she's too cool for them or something. Always off in her own world, not really interested in all the chick stuff they always do together. Karyn says—"

Reed stops as both he and Jeremy hear Karyn Aufiero,

the very person Reed's talking about, break out into her very distinct, infectious laugh. Reed and Jeremy glance diagonally across the room and spot Karyn, sitting on the edge of the couch, bent over as she cracks up over something.

Jeremy glances at Reed, taking in the way his friend is watching Karyn. It's like he's in a trance or something when he gazes at her—eyes intent, mouth fixed in a straight line. Jeremy stuffs his hands into his baggy pants pockets, feeling a twinge of sympathy for Reed. He's seen Reed look at Karyn like this before, and it's not tough to figure out what's up. But Reed's in a particularly difficult situation. Aside from the fact that Reed would risk ruining his friendship with Karyn if he ever told her how he felt, there is one other obstacle. Karyn is going out with Reed's older brother, T. J. And Jeremy knows Reed well enough to realize that Reed would never do anything to hurt T.J. No way. He'd rather stand on the sidelines and suffer.

Jeremy clears his throat in an attempt to subtly bring Reed back to the present. It works and Reed abruptly glances back at Jeremy.

"Oh, sorry," he says, rubbing the back of his neck. His mouth draws up into a crooked smile. "I was just thinking that we have to do something about that laugh of Karyn's. It's horrible."

Jeremy smiles and nods, knowing that Reed actually loves pretty much everything about the girl.

"Anyway," Reed says. "What was I saying again? Oh. Yeah. Meena. Someone should talk to her."

"Yeah, but not you, of course," Jeremy jokes.

"Nah. I think it's more of a girl thing," Reed says. "Too touchy-feely for me."

Jeremy just looks at Reed for a moment, thinking how funny it is that guys never, ever, under any circumstances, get to talk about anything deeper than sports and sex. Reed is definitely Jeremy's best friend, but he is sure there is a lot the two of them don't know about each other.

Then again, it would probably suck to be a girl. They all seem to know *everything* about one another.

"So, it doesn't look like anyone from Kennedy showed," Jeremy says finally. Reed nods. "Hey—want another beer?" Jeremy blurts out. "I think I'm going to get one."

"Yeah, okay." Reed walks with Jeremy toward the keg. Yes, Jeremy knows that a couple of minutes ago, a beer sounded like a bad idea. But Jeremy doesn't spend much time dwelling on his quick shift of heart. After all, that's just how life is. You have to run with it.

• • •

"Look at this lady." Keith laughs as he tailgates an old white Saab, maneuvering his huge Land Rover right up behind the little sedan. "I bet she starts crying or something."

Peter leans forward and squints to take a look at the woman driving the Saab. She does appear to be slightly panicked—from Peter's vantage point he can see the woman's eyes dart repeatedly to her rearview mirror; she's clearly uncomfortable with how close Keith's car is to hers.

29

Keith is just screwing with her and she finally seems to sense this, quickly switching over to the right lane.

"Knew you'd get her," Max says, staring down at the red-haired woman as both cars stop at a red light.

"Yeah, she was an easy target," Keith responds. He hits the gas hard as the light turns green and Peter lurches forward. "P., remember that grandma woman last year? That one who tried to give me a lecture through her closed window?" Keith asks Peter, glancing back at him.

Peter nods, even though he has no idea what Keith is talking about. "Yeah. That was funny." The lie comes easily enough for Peter. After all, lying is all Peter's done so far tonight. Lying and pretending—pretending he's having fun. Pretending he's as into riding around town with his friends as he used to be.

Keith and Max are laughing about something. Peter sits back in his seat and continues to tune out. He tugs on the collar of his T-shirt, trying to figure out why he's not having a good time. He was looking forward to tonight. And it sure beats sitting at home, watching crappy sitcoms or second-rate TV movies. But for some reason—and Peter doesn't know why—*this,* this aimless driving around, is not doing it for him. He knows that Keith and Max have not changed at all, but tonight Peter is having a hard time just hanging out with them like he used to. It's almost as if Peter lost a part of himself when he lost feeling in his legs. Exactly what he lost, Peter's not sure—his sense of humor? His ability to be with other people? To connect?

Be normal? Peter doesn't know. He just knows he feels empty. Numb. And alone.

At least he *can* feel a buzz from the two beers he's guzzled. That takes the edge off.

"Hey, I think Bozo's working at Mobil tonight," Max bursts out, pulling Peter out of his self-pity session. "Let's go rip him off."

Keith glances at the clock on the central console. "You're right. The jackass is definitely on duty. Let's do it." Keith makes a quick right, nearly taking out a young couple strolling down the street in the process.

Peter lays his head back against the seat, closing his eyes. "Bozo" the "jackass" is Bob, a clerk at the Mobil station's convenience store on the corner of Jones and Sycamore. Peter and his friends have ripped the guy off endless times over the past year. It's a cinch to steal when that dude's on the job. But right now, the idea of shoplifting at the gas station isn't all that appealing to Peter. It might have something to do with the fact that he can't run. Or walk, for that matter. What's he supposed to do after he swipes a six-pack? *Wheel* himself away? Even superslow Bob would be able to catch up with him.

Peter's friends haven't even considered this, however. They're yapping away as Keith drives toward the gas station, trying to decide what they feel like stealing tonight. Peter lifts his head back up and opens his eyes. He watches them, incredulous. When are they going to get it through their thick heads that he's paralyzed?

31

Maybe that's why I'm not into hanging out with them, Peter thinks, cracking his knuckles. *Because they're idiots.*

Keith pulls into the parking lot behind the convenience store. The lot is empty; there are no other cars around.

"Perfect," Keith says. He glances back at Peter, and his expression quickly changes—his features become heavier. His brown eyes darken.

Peter feels like he can see his friend thinking. Putting two and two together. Remembering that not everything is the same as it used to be.

"Oh. Maybe you should, I mean—" Keith begins. He scratches the back of his neck. Looks at Peter's legs, then quickly glances away.

"I'll stay here," Peter supplies, not able to stand this a second longer. He sees the pity start to creep back into Keith's eyes. The pity is so strong, it practically clouds Keith's glasses, making Peter feel about one centimeter tall.

"You sure?" Max asks.

Peter forces a laugh. "Don't think you'll make much of a getaway with me wheeling behind you." His two friends smile at this and Peter is relieved. He needs to blast all traces of their sympathy away. "Go ahead. I'll rate your performance from here. And take a little extra for me."

Max nods. "Oh, we will. Don't worry 'bout that."

Keith wiggles his eyebrows as he pops open his door. "See you in a few."

"I'll be counting down," Peter responds, gripping the edge of the car seat. It takes a lot out of him to force his enthusiasm like this. But his friends seem to have no idea that it's all an act. They both jump out of the car, heading for the store.

Peter finishes off his beer as he watches them go, that now familiar feeling of emptiness overcoming him. He fidgets with the aluminum can, denting it in the middle. The thing is, the fact that he can't join in is not the only reason Peter isn't digging this particular activity. He's got other things to think about. Things that matter.

Like how to get through life now that he can't take care of himself.

Like these bizarre dreams he's been having ever since the accident.

It all makes his friends' particular brand of fun seem kind of . . . pointless.

Peter looks away from the window. He tosses the beer can with the others, on the floor to the left of him. This is all he's wanted to do for days, and now that he's actually here, he just wants to go home. What the hell is wrong with him?

• • •

"Meena, are you all right?"

She looks up too fast and another wave of nausea slams through her. Luke's image swims above and she squeezes her eyes shut, presses her hands into the carpeted floor at her sides.

"A little queasy," she says. She's sweating. She feels disgusting, inside and out.

"Well, I know you haven't been drinking," Luke says with a laugh. "Eaten anything lately?"

Her stomach growls audibly the moment Luke says the word *eaten* and Meena's brow wrinkles. *Has* she eaten lately? Now that she thinks about it, she realizes she hasn't had anything since lunch early that afternoon. Her stomach has been so tied up in knots, it hasn't even occurred to her to eat.

Luke reaches down with one of his long, lanky arms, offering her his hand. Crooked under his other arm is a six-pack of beer. "C'mon," he says. "You need some fresh air."

"I don't want to go downstairs," Meena half whines, thinking of Justin and the fact that she'd rather shave herself bald than ever face him again.

"So we'll go out on the roof," Luke says. He tilts his head toward his bedroom and raises his eyebrows.

Meena likes the sound of that. She's spent a lot of time out on Luke Waller's roof over the last few years, much to the chagrin of his parents, who are constantly fretting over potential injuries and lawsuits. But somehow they've always been a little bit more concerned with making Luke's friends think they're cool than with safety, and so they allow it. Meena has always found it's a perfect place to chill, relax, take her mind off finals, big meets . . . guys.

She reaches up and Luke clasps her hand, pulling her to a standing position with one effortless tug. Meena gets a violent head rush and leans into Luke until it passes and she can walk on her own.

"Hey. Where are you guys going?"

Meena and Luke turn to find Dana emerging from the hall bathroom, closing the door behind her.

34

"Where do you think?" Luke says with a burp. "Come with."

Dana smiles. "Cool. I could use some quality time with the stars."

A couple of minutes later Meena, Luke, and Dana are sitting on the level part of the roof just outside Luke's bedroom window. Meena takes a deep breath, thinking about how much she loves it out here. She's always loved it out here, but tonight she relishes it—the sprawling star-filled sky above, the new perspective on life down below on the ground, the refreshing breeze flowing through her long hair and chilling her uncovered arms. . . . Meena almost feels like she's stepped out of her own life and has inhabited someone else's.

Luke sits between the two girls and rips off a beer. "Don't suppose I can offer you one," he says to Meena.

She opens her mouth to say no but instead finds herself staring at the glistening can. Other than the few sips of wine she's had in the last few weeks, she's really never consumed alcohol. Never been drunk. She always thought her friends looked so stupid when they were falling all over themselves, doing things they'd never otherwise do.

But if it took away your inhibitions, maybe it took away other stuff, too. Like fear. Like embarrassment. Like guilt.

Meena silently reaches out and takes the beer, popping the top before she can think about it any further.

"Hallelujah!" Luke shouts as Meena takes a sip.

"I do not believe what I'm seeing," Dana chimes in.

"That's disgusting," Meena says after one bitter swallow, wiping the back of her hand across her mouth.

Luke laughs and slaps her on the back. "The first one's always the hardest," he says. "Here. Just do it like me."

He pops open a can, leans his head back, and pours the whole thing down his throat without stopping for a breath.

Meena looks down at the can in her hands, the vile taste still stinging the inside of her mouth. *What are you doing?* the little voice in her mind shouts.

"Shutting you up," Meena answers under her breath.

She tilts her head back, closes her eyes, and starts to swallow. She only gets about half the can down before she has to stop to prevent herself from choking, but it's a start. When Meena looks at Dana again, Meena's smiling.

Dana, however, is not.

"What?" Meena says. "You guys have been dying to get me drunk for years."

"And you've never even sipped," Dana says. "Which is why I'm worried."

Meena's heart twists in her chest at Dana's serious tone. Dana hardly ever gets serious, so when she does, there's definitely something worth talking about. At least in Dana's opinion.

"Here we go," Luke says with an exaggerated roll of the eyes, apparently recognizing Dana's tone as well. "Buzz kill time." He pushes himself up and walks over to the edge of the roof, looking down at the partyers who have started to spill into the backyard.

Meena downs the rest of the beer, resisting the now familiar urge to vomit.

"I'm serious, Meena," Dana says. "You've been acting weird all night, we hardly see you anymore, and now you're drinking? What the heck is going on with you?"

"What do you mean, you hardly see me anymore?" Meena says, knowing exactly what Dana is referring to. The fact that she hasn't been Miss Social lately. The fact that she's been spending her time with . . . other people.

"I *mean* I was actually shocked when you said you wanted to come out tonight," Dana says. "I think you've been to, like, *one* party this year."

Suddenly Meena's jittery nervousness is back again. The beer is not working. Or maybe it's just not working fast enough. She grabs another one and takes a swig.

"So. What are you, my social secretary now?" she blurts out. Her foot is bouncing up and down uncontrollably.

"There's no reason to get all bitchy," Dana says indignantly. "I'm just trying to look out for you."

"Well, thanks for your concern!" Meena says, throwing her free hand up. "I don't believe this! Everyone's always picking on me because I don't drink and now that I am, you're all over me."

Meena can't believe what she's hearing herself say. She sounds like a baby. Like the baby everyone thinks she is. She wishes she could tell them. Wishes she could shout it from the rooftop—literally. I'm not innocent little Meena Miller anymore!

37

"Forget it," Dana says, shaking her head and looking away. "You're totally missing the point."

"Fine, I'll forget it," Meena says. She's on the verge of tears and she has no idea why. Everything is fine. No. More than fine. Everything is great. Things are happening. They're happening just the way she wants them to. So what if her friends don't get it? So what if it's impossible to explain? She should be happy.

She looks down at the beer in her hand and one tear spills over, sliding down her cheek as a stiff breeze nearly knocks the wind out of her.

I should be happy, she thinks. But she's not. In fact, all she's feeling at the moment is sorry for herself. And sickened by who she is.

Tilting her head back, Meena downs the rest of the beer. So what if it's not working yet? She'll just keep drinking until it does.

CHAPTER THREE

Meena is treading water. She's treading water in what seems to be an ocean, and her calf muscles are getting tired. Exhausted. She doesn't know how much longer she can stay afloat, but as she looks around, straining to lift her head above the water, above the waves, she doesn't see a person in sight.

Meena's throat burns from the saltiness, but at least the ocean is warm. At least she's not going to freeze to death. The sun is out. It's beating down hard, in fact. Meena closes her eyes and tilts her head, enjoying the way the rays of sun are caressing her cheeks and forehead. Maybe this isn't so bad. Maybe she can just back float and stay out here a long time.

But when Meena opens her eyes, she sees something floating downstream toward her. An object. Meena's heartbeat picks up as the shiny object comes closer. And closer. Finally it floats close enough for Meena to see it clearly. She gasps, swallowing water as she does so.

She has to get away. She has to get away now.

Meena is choking from the swallowed salt water, but she turns and swims away as fast as she can just the same.

Her legs couldn't be more tired, but she swims as hard and as fast as she can, funneling all of her energy into her arms. She swims the way she does in meets, with complete focus and determination, barely lifting her head from the water.

Finally, out of breath, Meena does lift her head. She looks back. It's still there. In fact, it's getting closer.

Terrified, Meena dives down and swims underwater, her heart beating in her ears. She pushes her way through seaweed and algae—some of it clings to her. It's slimy and she wants to shake it off, but she has no time for that. She needs to focus on swimming as far as possible. When she can't hold her breath any longer, she reluctantly swims back up to the surface.

But when Meena pops her head out of the water, all she sees is a small raft. She smiles, relieved, and immediately reaches for the red plastic boat. A hand thrusts out to grab hers. At first Meena is grateful and she takes the hand. But the moment she touches his skin, she knows that it is him.

Meena quickly recoils her hand, but his only reaches out farther, trying to grasp her again, so she plunges downward, needing to get as far away from his hand—from him—as possible.

This time Meena sinks to the bottom of the ocean. Her feet touch the sand. She's surprised that even though she's submerged in the sea, she has no trouble breathing. Still petrified, Meena tries to calm herself down. She takes slow breaths. Closes her eyes. Then she looks around.

Suddenly right before her sits Harris Driver. Meena's knees buckle from the shock and she falls, all the while staring right into Harris's blue eyes.

He looks exactly like he did when he was ten, freckles and all. Meena is terrified and confused and is about to ask him what he's doing here when he opens his mouth and says: "It's all your fault." His voice is distorted from the water, but Meena is certain that's what he's saying.

"It's all your fault."

Meena's eyes fly open. The minute she spots her swimming medals on the shelves across from her bed, she knows it was just a nightmare. But her heart is racing, and she's sweating.

The fact that this was all in her head doesn't make her any less scared. It makes her more scared, actually. Meena sits up and leans against the wall next to her bed. She grabs the edge of her light gray curtain and squeezes it. Her head feels like it weighs two tons and her mouth feels dry and scratchy, as if she really did swallow salt water. She must be hung over. All that beer . . .

Meena peeks behind the curtain. She squints—the late morning sunlight is too much for her and she lets the drapes fall back into place.

Meena knows that she doesn't want to do anything today other than sit in bed. She feels too tired. And achy. And scared. And depressed. She's too drained to stay awake but too terrified to sleep.

• • •

It's late Sunday morning and Danny Chaiken is lost in his own zone. Not lost so much as reveling in it. Thriving. His eyes are closed, his body is jamming, and his spirits are soaring as the rap music pumps into his ears.

41

Danny's aware that the CD he's rocking out to at the Sunshine Records' listening station is a cheap Eminem rip-off, but he doesn't care. It's the first time Danny's heard this album and he's always psyched to hear something new. He lives for this stuff.

Danny's eyes are scrunched shut, his hands are playing out the beat against the legs of his baggy black pants, and his lips are mouthing the lyrics that he's already learned.

Don't try to understand me / I just be what I gotta be / Bust loose and set me free. . . .

Danny may be in the middle of the Winetka Falls Mall, his feet may be tapping against the music store's shiny wood floors, but it doesn't matter. Mentally Danny's in the song. He can see the dude rapping right before him, with his pink hair and three trillion piercings and everything, and suddenly Danny imagines himself to be the musician—he's the one up there onstage—all the hot girls in the audience want him and all the guys want to be him, and Danny is feeling the energy and love vibes in a major way. He would treat his fans better than a lot of other rappers or rock stars do, of course. He'd really hang with them and answer their letters and tell them what it's like, what it's *really* like, and—

"'Scuse me? Record hog? I think someone else wants to listen to this."

Danny jumps, opening his eyes as Cori Lerner whips the headphones off his head. He glances around—to the right, to the left, behind Cori. Not a person in sight. He does spot Karyn Aufiero and Amy Santisi, two of their classmates, over by some of the displays full of chick-music CDs, and he gives them a friendly wave hello. Karyn and Amy are fairly cool as far as cheerleaders go.

Then Danny turns his attention back to Cori. "Who?" he asks.

Cori smiles and her already insanely bright blue eyes brighten even more. "Okay. Fine," she says. She places the headphones back on their little metal stand, to the right of Danny, and she comes so close that Danny can smell her perfume or her shampoo or whatever it is that's making her smell so damn good. She smells like rain. Danny stuffs his hands into his pockets. How do they bottle rain, anyway?

"No one's waiting," Cori admits. "Just me. I'm ready to go. You've listened to every new album like three times already."

Danny grins and shakes his head, rubbing at the back of his neck. If this was any other female—Danny's mom, one of his sisters, even another one of his girl friends—the comment would piss him off. After all, Danny lives, breathes, and dreams music. But with Cori, it's different. She's a musicphile, too, so he knows that even though she's mocking him and making him leave, she understands his obsession. And she probably only wants to leave to snag some of those curly fries she's addicted to.

"I don't know what kind of DJ you are," Danny says, taking on a tone of mock disappointment.

"The best kind," Cori shoots back. "You should see the list of gigs I have lined up."

Probably has as much to do with your looks as your spinning ability, Danny thinks. Unfair of him, maybe, because she is a kick-ass DJ, but it's universally recognized by the guys in Danny's circle that there's nothing sexier than Cori Lerner behind the turntable. In fact, in Danny's opinion, there's nothing sexier than Cori standing in the middle of the music store. Suddenly Danny realizes he's probably inappropriately staring at her and tries to remember what they were talking about. *Her gigs. Right.*

"Whatever," Danny says, rolling his eyes. The pause in conversation was actually brief enough for him to cover. "I mean, *real* DJs want to hear every song as soon as they come out." Despite Danny's teasing, he steps away from the listening station and starts to follow Cori out of the store. As Cori walks ahead, he finds himself staring at a smooth-looking band of exposed skin right above her butt, at the place where her black T-shirt and her gray hip hugger pants don't quite meet. *Man.* Hip hugger pants are the best.

Cori glances over her shoulder and rolls her eyes as she walks through Sunshine Records' revolving door. Danny quickly averts his own eyes so that she doesn't see where he was staring. He's blushing a bit as he circles his way out of the exit, but Cori doesn't seem to notice.

"DJs do not go to the *mall* to listen to music," she informs Danny. "The cheesy atmosphere kills the vibe. Besides, why leave home when you can download new music in the comfort of your own room?"

Danny is so distracted by watching Cori's full, dark red lips move that he almost misses everything she says. Almost.

He clears his throat, falling in step next to Cori as she begins to walk. "Don't think I can agree with you there, lady," he says. His voice sounds deep, raspy, and burnt—a perfect imitation of Jethro, the afternoon DJ on 93.6, Winetka Falls' alternative radio station. "The sound quality on the download just is not up to par with that of a CD. At least not yet. You dig?"

Cori busts out laughing and she has to stop walking for a moment to catch her breath. You wouldn't think a girl like Cori—a girl who's never read *Seventeen* magazine, never purchased a bottle of pink nail polish, never watched a single nanosecond of *Dawson's Creek*—you wouldn't think a girl like that would actually giggle. But she does, and every time it drives Danny a little more crazy—in a good way. And the fact that she laughs at his jokes? That's just icing on the cake.

"You sound exactly like him," Cori says. Composing herself, she pulls down on her T-shirt and pushes her hair—dyed black with a few strategically placed red streaks—behind her ears, then begins to walk again. "I mean, exactly."

Walking beside Cori, Danny shrugs casually, though on the inside he's jumping up and down from the compliment. He's doing freakin' cartwheels. "That's what you get from listening to the radio twenty-four seven."

"No, come on," Cori says. She jabs at Danny's stomach, and a rush of excitement zigzags through his skinny body. "That's a serious talent."

Danny doesn't know what to do, so he just shrugs again. Even though he loves getting compliments—loves it, right up there with composing songs and performing in a play—he never knows how to react to them. So he doesn't.

"Okay. Question," he says, stopping in his tracks as they near the up escalator. "Where are we going?"

Cori lifts one eyebrow—the one with the tiny silver hoop—the one that Danny has fantasized many, many times about kissing, and then he's off again, daydreaming about the moment when it will actually, finally happen. . . .

"Danny?" Cori asks, snapping her fingers in front of his face. "You with me? Do you want fries or what?"

Danny blinks, then shakes his head, running a hand through his scruffy dark blond hair. He shifts his weight from one foot to the other, feeling stupid. "Did you ask me that already? Sorry. Zoned out for a second."

Cori crosses her toned arms over her chest. She looks up at Danny through long, dark eyelashes. "I see. Good thing I wasn't telling you anything important—just that I wanted to go to the food court. I'm dealing with a serious french fry craving."

Danny nods. He still feels a little dumb about being a total space case and has the urge to go splash some cold water on his face in order to wake himself up. Stay focused. "Gotcha. I'm gonna duck into the bathroom. Meet you up there?"

"Sure," Cori says. "I'll be the one scarfing down a jumbo-size fries."

46

Danny points a finger at her and says in his Jethro imitation: "Catch you on the flip side."

Cori laughs again, and as Danny watches her get on the escalator, he feels jittery and high and all charged up. Superpsyched. This is what hanging with Cori does to him and he's not sure if it's a good thing. Well, obviously it's a good thing, but the point is—

Danny snaps out of his racing thoughts as he realizes he's just standing in the middle of the mall like an idiot. Forcing people to maneuver around him. Time to get that cold water treatment, pronto. Tugging on his silver chain necklace, Danny heads straight for the men's room and goes to one of the sinks, splashing water on his face.

Danny doesn't know when he got in the habit of doing this, this whole water routine, and he would never admit that he does it to anyone. But for some reason, it works. Gets his thoughts back in line. Clears his head. And definitely calms his hormones down.

Feeling refreshed, rejuvenated, Danny shuts off the water and grabs a paper towel from the dispenser, wiping his face dry. A few cool drops fall to his green T-shirt, and he pulls the front away from his chest, shaking it out as he steps in front of the mirror.

His face freezes as he looks at his reflection.

So. It's not enough that his skin is paler than a baby's behind, not enough that he got visited by the freckle fairy one too many times, not enough that he has the face of an eleven-year-old. No. He also has to get a huge, nasty, pus-filled zit smack-dab in the middle of his left cheek.

Danny places his hands down on the porcelain sink, leaning forward to get a closer look. Obviously Cori has seen this zit. There's no way she could miss it. How could she? Danny's grip tightens on the sink as he gets pissed off. Very pissed off.

Danny might not be the best-looking guy in Winetka Falls, but he's always had okay skin. No zits, no pimples. That is, until freakin' Dr. Lansky, the shrink that Danny's been forced to see since June, put him on hellish combinations of pills. He's already switched his medication twice. These pills are supposed to help Danny but only end up giving him screwed-up side effects. Like acne.

Danny feels like screaming. Like ripping the paper towel dispenser off the wall. He was fine before he saw Lansky. More than fine. And he never got zits.

The bathroom door swings open and two college-age-looking guys walk in. Danny steps away from the sink. But he can't stop himself from taking one more long look in the mirror, trying to figure out if there's any way that he can cover this damn pimple up. But the thing is too massive. And he knows he has to get going. Cori has probably finished her fries by now.

Danny hangs his head as he slumps out of the bathroom. His face burns and he feels like everyone is staring at him. Laughing at him. Look at that skinny kid with the huge zit, they're saying.

But by the time Danny gets upstairs to the food court,

he's calmed himself down a bit. Enough, at least, so that he can function and manage a conversation with Cori. And he's figured out how he's going to handle this whole pimple thing with her.

He spots Cori right away. She's sitting at a table next to the balcony, sipping soda from a straw, a partially eaten bag of fries on the small square table in front of her. She sits back in her seat as Danny drops down across from her. He immediately pulls one of her many napkins across the table, snags the pen out of his pocket, and starts to draw one of the monster faces he's been habitually drawing since he was about ten. Doodling is one thing Danny's always been able to rely on to relieve his nervous tension.

"Did you fall in or something?" Cori asks.

Danny shakes his head, gives her his best smile, and says, "No. I was battling this thing." He pauses in his doodling and points to his zit. "Which I got, just so you know, because of Ritalin. I never get zits. I am not a zit boy. Not me."

Cori laughs. One of her reddish streaks of hair falls in front of her right eye and she pushes it away. "All right. Guess I'll steer clear of the Ritalin, then."

Danny grabs a fry and pops it into his mouth, the little monster drawing forgotten. "That would be a wise decision."

He chews and swallows slowly, trying to gulp down the lump that has formed in his throat as well. The lump that always forms in his throat when he has to lie about himself. When he feels like he has so much to hide, he's not even sure if he knows what all the secrets are.

"Does it have a lot of side effects?" Cori asks, her voice curious. Not concerned, which is good. Danny hates concern.

"Eh, you know, not really," he says quickly. "Where did you say you were spinning this weekend? Maybe I'll come."

Cori's face changes ever so slightly and it's clear she's worried she's made Danny uncomfortable. Great. Now he feels guilty for making her feel bad. But what was he supposed to say?

Actually, I don't know what the side effects of Ritalin are because I've never been on Ritalin because people with ADD are put on Ritalin and contrary to what everyone at school thinks, I don't have ADD. No, what I have is a lot more rare. And a lot more freakish. And you might as well just write me off right now.

"I'm gonna be at Clyde's on Saturday night," Cori says, and Danny's heart warms because she doesn't press, she doesn't apologize. She simply takes the hint and goes with the topic shift. "You should definitely show."

Danny smiles, relieved. "Sounds good," he says, the tension fading quickly. He goes back to his doodling, putting the final touches on the hideous face he's created.

• • •

On Sunday afternoon, as Meena drives herself across town for yet another night of baby-sitting, she has the music turned up so loud in her car, people walking on the street are stopping to glare at her. Meena, however, barely notices. She has to keep singing at the top of her lungs to come close to being able to ignore the pounding of her heart. She has to keep singing to drown out her thoughts.

"I did it! Do you think I've gone too far? I did it! Guilty as charged!" she practically screams along with Dave Matthews. Then she suddenly hears what she's actually singing and her breath catches in her throat. She turns off the radio, cuts the wheel, and slams on the brakes, screeching to a stop in the Claytons' driveway.

Both cars are there. That's good. That's a start. Her hands shaking uncontrollably, Meena puts the car in reverse and pulls out again, then parks her Honda CRX against the curb so that the Claytons can get their cars out.

Meena looks up at the house, so utterly unassuming and normal. She takes in the brightly lit windows, the flowered curtains that hang downstairs, the bright blue door that Steven Clayton painted last spring and is so proud of because it's different from every other door on the block. Meena smirks, remembering the day he pointed it out to her, all satisfied smiles. Then her stomach lurches and she has to close her eyes.

"Take a deep breath," she tells herself, and does. "All is well."

Then, as if she believes this statement, she gets out of the car, tosses her long dark hair behind her shoulder, and walks up the front path to the door, chin held high. It takes some effort, but it is held high.

The Claytons, both of them, open the door mere seconds after the doorbell chimes. Meena's eyes focus on

Lydia Clayton's face. The warm brown eyes. The tiny little wrinkles in her forehead. The birthmark just left of her nose. Lydia is talking. She's saying something about Trace having the slightest of colds. But Meena isn't hearing it. She's too busy concentrating on not looking at Steven.

Steven, who is hovering just behind his wife's shoulder. Steven, who, Meena can tell from the corner of her eye, is trying to catch her gaze. Steven, who, if she looks at him, will undoubtedly smile that smile. That you're-my-special-girl smile. Meena clenches her fists to try to ward off the morbid urge to look. But if she looks, Lydia will notice. If she looks, Lydia will know.

I kissed a married man, Meena thinks as Lydia finishes her speech. *I kissed your husband.*

And then she looks. And there it is. The private smile that's just for her. The private smile that always makes her heart soar. Impulsively, grotesquely, Meena's lips start to twitch. She's going to smile back.

But then Lydia's hand reaches out and finds Steven's. His fingers close around hers. His wife's. His wife's hand with the matching wedding band.

Meena presses her hand into the doorjamb to prevent herself from crumbling.

"Are you okay, honey?" Lydia says, reaching up with her free hand to touch Meena's clammy cheek. "You look pale. Do you want some water?"

At a loss for what else to do, Meena feels herself nod. She follows the Claytons, hand in hand, into their house, staring at the entwined fingers. Noticing the way their arms swing just slightly, like a couple of teenagers still giddy over the fact that they've started holding hands.

This is wrong, this is wrong, this is wrong, Meena thinks. And suddenly something hits her in the stomach with the force of a wrecking ball. The realization of what she's done. The final realization that her nerves don't stem from the fear of getting caught. They don't stem from the excitement of the affair. They come from something much, much darker.

I'm seventeen, she thinks. *I'm just a kid. I didn't want to think so. I wanted to believe him that I'm different, older. But I'm just a stupid skinny kid, and he's an adult. An adult with a wife. And a kid of his own.*

Meena's knees give out, but luckily by this time she's standing in front of a kitchen chair. Lydia is getting her a glass of water from the refrigerator, her back to the room. Meena's eyes slowly travel up to meet Steven's and his are shining. Shining as he looks down at his "special" girl.

A thick, black layer of disgust encloses Meena's heart and she looks away, her eyes blinded by hot tears.

• • •

Jeremy knows that most people would never consider filing to be fun. And he doesn't exactly, either. But on a day like this one—a lazy, overcast Sunday with nothing but homework facing him at his house—Jeremy does find it to be relaxing in a mind-numbing sort of way. Especially when he and Josh Strauss, who's entering data into the computer in the corner, have a boom box tuned to 93.6 and are joking around and laughing as they work.

"Yes! Three piles done," Jeremy says. He leans back in his chair and stretches out his long arms. He drops his hands down flat on the armrests and eyes all the papers that are still stacked on the desk in front of him. "Only about three hundred more to go."

Josh laughs, glancing over at Jeremy. "I'll trade you. I only have about a thousand more names to enter."

Jeremy shakes his head. "No thanks, man." He picks up Lonnie Pierce's paperwork and bends down to drop it into the red-labeled *P* folder. "Think I'll stick to the files here."

"Look at my industrious son," Jeremy's mother says as she comes strolling into the office, her brown heels clicking against the wooden floor. She walks right over to Jeremy and gives his shoulders a little massage. "How's it going?"

Jeremy swivels his chair around so that he's looking right at his mom. Sometimes she really does amaze him. It's Sunday, she works at a halfway house of all places, and she's completely put together and semiglamorous looking. Not that Jeremy is complaining. She always looks great and is always laid-back, and Jeremy's the only one of his friends who *isn't* embarrassed to have his mom around when he's got people over.

"Fine," Jeremy responds. "I think I'll be done sometime this decade."

Jeremy's mom smiles, pushing her thick red hair behind her shoulders. "As long as you're done by graduation, we'll be okay." She walks over to her desk by the window and grabs a manila folder, hugging it to her chest. "Hey. I didn't get to talk with you this morning. How was the party?"

Jeremy goes back to his filing. "Pretty cool."

"Good. And you, Josh? Did you do anything fun last night?" Jeremy's mom asks.

"Not really. Just went to the mall," Josh responds. "Oh, but hey—" He stops and looks over at Jeremy. "This girl from my school, Bria Haymes, is having a huge party Friday night. You should come."

"Oh yeah? What's the deal?" Jeremy asks.

Josh glances warily over at Jeremy's mom.

"All right. I think I'll make my exit now," Jeremy's mom says, holding up her hands and laughing. "I'll let you boys talk about things you'd rather not discuss in front of a mother."

She pulls open the door and walks out, reminding Jeremy of exactly why his mom is so great. She totally gives him and his friends space to do their own thing.

"Your parents are so cool," Josh says. He stands, walks over to Jeremy's desk, and leans back against it. "Anyway, yeah, Bria's parents are going to be out of town. It'll be massive."

"I can deal with that." Jeremy's stomach grumbles and he looks at his watch. Tara should be here any minute to meet him for lunch.

Right on cue, the office door opens and Tara walks in. Jeremy smiles. There are moments, like this one, where he seriously thinks they have something telepathic going on.

"Hey, babe," he says, standing up to go give Tara a quick kiss. She smells like pears and baby powder.

"Hi," she says. She hooks her arm through his and looks around the room. "Seems like you guys are busy. Have you worked up an appetite?"

"You have no idea." Jeremy glances over at Josh. "Tara, this is Josh, Josh, Tara," he says, taking a step away from Tara as she stretches out her hand to his friend.

"Hi," Tara says with an easy smile. "Jeremy's told me a lot about you."

Josh grins. He sticks a hand in the back pocket of his corduroys. "What's he told you? That I'm a slacker who makes him listen to techno every now and then?"

"No," Tara responds. Her big brown eyes are playful as she takes Jeremy's arm again. "He's only told me good things."

"Yeah. And you're lucky, considering how horrible that techno is," Jeremy says, nudging Josh with the elbow that Tara has not latched onto.

A weird, vague vibe of discomfort swims through Jeremy. He clears his throat and looks at Tara. "Josh was just telling me about this huge Kennedy party on Friday night. Wanna go?"

Tara bites her lip. "I can't, sweetie," she says. Her cell phone starts to ring and she releases her arm from Jeremy's so that she can fish through her purse. "I'm having a girls' night, remember?" By the time Tara finds her phone, it's stopped ringing. "Damn," she says quietly. "But you should go without me." She pushes the button to listen to her voice mail and holds the phone up to her ear.

"Yeah," Josh says. "Feel free to tag along. I'm gonna head over there with Chris Demay. You know him, right?"

"Um, yeah. From football." Jeremy fingers his gold chain, fiddling with the pendant that is in the shape of his jersey number—3. "Nice guy."

"So you wanna come with us?"

Jeremy looks at Tara, who's still listening to her message. She's going to be busy Friday night, anyway, so he might as well go. And he does like the idea of going to another school's rager, seeing an entirely new scene.

Jeremy glances back at Josh, wondering why the invitation isn't sitting right. Maybe the fact that it's a *Kennedy* party—Falls' biggest rival—is bugging him out a little. Does he really want to deal with seeing someone like Sam Dowager when he doesn't have to?

But then, the party does sound like fun. . . .

Tara finally clicks off the phone and Jeremy tells Josh, "I'll let you know later in the week. Right now I'm so hungry, I can barely think."

"Sure," Josh says. "Whatever."

"Well, let's get some lunch, then," Tara says. She tugs on Jeremy's arm, pulling him toward the door. "Bye, Josh. Nice to meet you!"

"You too. Later," Josh calls as they walk out of the office.

Once Jeremy and Tara are in the carpeted hallway and are on their way down the stairs, Tara grasps Jeremy's arm as if she just remembered something. "Oh! Should we have invited Josh to come with us?" she asks, her dark eyebrows furrowed.

"No," Jeremy responds quickly. So quickly that Tara gives him a funny look. "I mean, I worked with him all morning. I want to spend time with you alone."

Tara seems satisfied with Jeremy's response. Satisfied enough that she gives him a kiss on the cheek.

And once Jeremy gets his hands on some pizza, he'll be satisfied, too.

• • •

Meena tries to knit as she sits in the Claytons' cluttered living room, as the Claytons' two-year-old son, Trace, sleeps calmly in his room, but it's no use. She's too wound up. Too on guard.

She gets up and walks over to the wall unit. Turns on the radio. It's tuned to a classical station and she leaves it—Meena's not listening for entertainment's sake, she just wants to drown out the overwhelming silence.

When Steven and Lydia left, they went out separately. And on nights when they go out separately, Steven usually comes home earlier than Lydia. Sometimes much earlier—Meena can never predict when. She used to look forward to these nights, knowing she'd have Steven alone for a few minutes, sometimes for hours. But this time it's different. This time she's dreading it.

Meena is sweating. It is always hot in this house. And stuffy. Meena inhales. She can still smell the smoke from the cigarette she put out five minutes ago. If Steven comes home now, he'll smell it, too. Every single nerve in Meena's body, every single muscle, tenses up. If Steven knows she was smoking here again, he'll be angry. He didn't like it when Meena picked up smoking a few weeks ago. Yet somehow she only does it when she's in his house or when she's home afterward. She's not even sure why she started. Made her feel older, maybe. More sophisticated. Was that why? She doesn't remember.

Meena has to put these thoughts out of her mind. She has to relax. So she focuses on the two pink knitting needles in her hands, on the blue-and-green scarf she's making in her lap. And for a moment she calms down and simply knits. Forgets where she is.

But then she hears the sound of a car driving up the street and she immediately remembers. She looks up, grasping tightly onto the cool metal needles—so tightly that her fingernails dig into the palms of her hands. Two bright headlights illuminate the front window.

Not tonight, she thinks. *I don't want to be alone with you tonight. I just want to go home.*

Just as quickly as the car comes, it passes, but Meena is still tense. She slowly releases her grip on the needles, then rubs her sweaty palms against her jeans. *You're such a baby,* the little voice in her head says. *You started this, now you'll have to deal with it.*

But had she started it? Yes, she'd had a crush on Steven ever since she was old enough to know what a crush was.

59

Yes, she'd fantasized about what it would be like to kiss him. But had she been the one who started the change in their relationship? Was it her fault? It had to be, didn't it? Because what kind of adult man would initiate a relationship with his friends' daughter—his son's *baby-sitter?* What kind of man would pursue a seventeen-year-old girl?

Her mind is racing, and her heart is beating fast, and once again Meena tells herself she has to calm down. She's just about to begin knitting again when the standing lamp, the one to the left of the brown couch she's sitting on, starts to flicker. The flicker is annoying, it gets under her skin the same way static on the radio does, so she stands and hits the switch to shut the lamp off.

It's a little bit darker now—the overhead light is pretty dim—but light enough for Meena to continue on with her knitting. She sits back down, crosses her legs Indian style, and picks up her needles.

Just as Meena is really starting to numb her mind in the repetitive rhythm of it, just as she's once again starting to forget that she's sick to her stomach, she hears the sound of another car coming down Laight Street.

Meena goes through the routine again. She grips the knitting needles. Looks up. Freezes as the headlights shine through the front window. This time those blaring lights don't pass. They come closer, shine even brighter, stay stationary for a moment.

And then they shut off, along with the sound of the car's engine.

Meena feels her heart rise up to her throat. She feels shaky and completely paralyzed, incapable of motion, at the same time. She hears the car door slam—the sound of that slam reverberates through her entire body.

Meena's view is blocked—she can't see the driver step out of the car, but then the house's outside light highlights something that flushes the nervousness right out of her: the car is white. Which means it has to be Lydia's Toyota. Not Steven's black Volvo.

Every part of Meena, even her eyeballs, seems to relax. *Lydia* is the one who came home early tonight. Meena gathers her knitting, stuffs it into the cream public television tote bag that her mother gave her. Lydia won't say anything about the cigarette smoke. She won't even notice it. She'll just want to go to sleep. Which means Meena can go home.

Meena hears the key jiggling in the lock, then hears the front door swing open. She stands and turns around, about to greet Lydia, but her stomach hits the floor and she shuts her mouth before any words come out. Because it's not Lydia standing in the front hall. It's Steven.

"Meena," he says. He tosses his jacket on the antique chair that sits by the stairs, then walks toward the living room. Toward Meena. "How's it going?"

Meena can barely speak, still reeling from the shock that she has to deal with Steven when she was expecting Lydia. She looks to the front window, at the white car illuminated under the light. "That's Lydia's car," she says quietly.

"Huh?" Steven strolls over to the couch. He plops

down right next to where Meena's standing. He looks over at the Toyota. "Oh—yeah. Lyd took the Volvo. She was going out with a bunch of friends and there's more room."

"Oh." Meena hugs the tote bag to her body. She barely looks at Steven. When she looks at him, she thinks about the kiss. And when she thinks about the kiss, she feels disgusting—unclean. She can't believe she was ever excited about this. When she remembers how light as air she was when she kissed him, she just wants to die. She has to get out of here. Now.

"Trace is asleep," she says, staring at the door. Then she ducks her head, letting her hair hide her face. "I'll let myself out."

She takes just one step when Steven says, "Hey. Come on. Aren't you going to hang out and talk for a moment?"

There's a plea in his voice. A disappointment. Meena knows that a week ago, she would have grinned at the realization that he wanted to be with her. Tonight it only makes her need for escape more acute.

She shakes her head—takes another step. "I'm tired. I need to go home."

Steven stands, leans over the couch, and reaches for her arm. "Come on," he says. "I thought you loved our little talks. I know I look forward to them every week." He only touches her lightly, but to Meena it feels like an ironclad grip. He moves closer, then his expression hardens into a slight frown. "Were you smoking again, Meena?" he asks, an edge to his voice.

"I need to go home," Meena repeats, ignoring his question. "I have to get up early tomorrow."

Steven looks at Meena for a long moment. "Don't dismiss me, Meena," he says quietly. "Not after what we've shared."

Meena's nerves sizzle, causing a miniquake within her own body.

"That kiss meant the world to me, Meena," Steven presses. "I thought it meant the same to you."

Meena looks in his eyes and her heart sinks. He has her. And he knows he does. There's so much need in his eyes. So much longing. And it's for her. Little Meena Miller. No longer a baby. She knows how he's going to touch her, and she dreads it with an intensity that nearly overwhelms her. But she feels powerless to stop it. He needs her. And she's made him need her. She did start this. She's here because she chose this. And there's no going back.

She hugs the bag closer to her chest, slowly makes her way back around the couch, and sits. As close to the battered armrest and as far from Steven as possible. Her heart is pounding and her body feels weak. More than anything in the world, she just wants to leave.

Steven quickly closes up the gap in space, scooting closer to Meena. "I knew you'd stay," he whispers in her ear, causing a chill down her neck that repulses her. "You need me as much as I need you."

Now that he's so near, Meena can smell the whiskey on his breath. Her hands clench onto her bag's frayed straps, and she stares down at the fading station logo printed on the front. She stares so hard that the picture becomes a fuzzy blur.

Get out, she thinks. *If you run, he won't catch you. Maybe he's drunk enough that he'll trip. Maybe he'll let you go.*

The tip of his finger travels down her cheek. Meena's heart is thumping so loudly, her pulse is racing so quickly, that she feels like she can actually visualize these bodily functions. She focuses on doing this—imagines her heart throbbing, pictures her blood running through her veins—so as to pull herself out of this moment and pretend this is not really happening.

"Meen?" Steven prods. "Aren't you going to say something?"

Meena slowly tilts her head to look at him. A sudden, powerful rush of anger washes over her, heats up her face. Her whole body. "I want to go home," she says. She means to sound strong, but her voice is shaky.

"Oh, Meen," Steven chides. His finger now traces her arm. She's wearing a long-sleeved sweatshirt as she always does when she baby-sits, but it still feels like Steven's touching her bare skin. "You do know how much I want you, don't you?"

Meena's breath catches. Terror takes over, controlling her. He can't mean—

"I've been waiting all weekend to see you," Steven says. He lifts his hand from her arm, runs it over her dark hair. He stares at Meena with pleading eyes.

Meena looks down at her lap again. "Don't," she says. The fear has her so out of breath that she feels like she has to use all of her energy to speak. To spit that one feeble word out.

"I only want to show you how much I care about you," Steven says. He pushes a strand of Meena's hair behind her ear, causing chills of repulsion to travel again down her shoulders and back. His other hand grips her waist—hard. And this time Meena knows she's not imagining the force of his strength. "Please let me be close to you, Meena. I need you . . . please."

But it's not a matter of letting him. The pain from his grip makes that very obvious. There is nothing she can do. She can't even breathe.

"You want me as much as I want you, Meena," he says. "I've seen it in your eyes. I felt it in your kiss. You're not as innocent as you want the world to believe."

Meena's eyes begin to cloud with tears. Nausea rises up in her stomach. She did let him kiss her. She did kiss him back. This is all her fault. She didn't want to be a baby anymore. And she's not.

She's a slut.

Steven leans in closer and starts to kiss the side of her neck. Behind her ear. Meena can feel the scratchiness of his unshaven face against her skin.

Tears fall down Meena's cheeks. She wants to tell Steven to stop. But she knows he's right. She is to blame. And he'll never let her leave.

"Oh, Meen," Steven whispers in her ear. His hand creeps over her stomach. Crawls toward her breast.

Every inch of Meena's skin prickles with fear. With horror. With hatred.

"I want you," he says.

Meena squeezes her eyes closed. She knows what is about to happen. Knows he's going to force his way inside her. And she knows she's powerless to stop it. Meena tries to drown everything out, shut it all off. She's defeated and scared out of her mind and there's nothing she can do.

So Meena does the only thing she can.

She tries not to feel a thing.

CHAPTER FOUR

Meena closes her eyes as the hot, hot water pounds against her face and chest. She is surrounded by steam in the shower stall; the glass door is all fogged up. She has been in here a very long time.

Ever since she got home from the Claytons'.

Her parents were in the kitchen when she arrived, and she ran past the open kitchen door as quickly as possible, calling out to them that she was going to take a quick shower.

"Okay, honey!" her mother called. The total normalcy in her tone almost made Meena trip and fall on the stairs. They had no idea what had happened to her. What had just happened to their precious baby. Their little Meena. And they'd never know.

Meena can hear muffled noises from below. The opening and closing of cabinets as her parents make a late supper together. She can hear, in her mind, their casual careless banter. But just thinking of her parents makes her stomach lurch dangerously.

What if they find out? What if they hate me? Meena's thoughts race forward. *What if they find out and they don't want me anymore?*

Meena grabs the big bar of soap and for the fourth time scrubs at her arms, her legs, behind her neck. But it's useless. She can't wipe away the shame. Can't rinse off that gut-wrenching guilt and self-hate that's eating away at her soul.

She can't get clean.

Meena knows this shower is useless. There's no way she's going to be able to scrub away the anger, the hurt, or the guilt. She reaches to turn the water off, to give up and get out of the shower, when the sheer horror and disgust of what happened tonight comes back to her in a rush.

Part of her can't believe he really did it. That this person she'd always admired and trusted—that he forced her. Raped her.

"I want you," he'd said.

Meena can still feel him inside her. She still feels sore and ripped open and humiliated and dirty and terrified. She begins to scrub again. Hard. So hard, it almost hurts. Her skin looks red and raw—from the hot water, from the scrubbing, from the shame.

"Oh God," Meena cries out. She drops the soap, feeling more helpless than she ever has in her life. She slides down the side of the shower, sits in the corner, and begins to cry.

She hugs her knees to her chest, watches the water come spouting out over her head, and wonders why. Why did this have to happen to her? Why did she *let this* happen?

Meena drops her head, clasps her hands behind her neck, and sobs. But even the sound of her cries can't drown out the sound of his voice inside her head.

"I know you want me, Meena," he says. *"I've seen the way you look at me. I know from the way you kissed me. You've made me want you. And you knew what you were doing. Admit it. You always knew."*

Meena lifts her head. Tries to focus through her tears on the blue and white octagonal tiles across from her. This is all her fault. She flirted. She smiled and blushed and lowered her eyes. So many times. So many lingering conversations. So many giggles and slight touches and smiles.

Slowly Meena stands. She lets out a shaky, stifled breath. Rubs at her eyes. And then she shuts the water off.

"You want me," he'd said as he slowly removed her clothes. *"You've shown me in so many ways, and that's why you won't stop me now. Why you can't. Because you want this, too."*

Meena knows that she is the one to blame. And that's why she can never tell. Not her parents. Not her friends. Not her brothers. Then they'll know. They'll know what a slut she is. That she's an adulterer. That she's dirty. Worthless.

She steps out of the shower and grabs her ratty yellow towel, wrapping it around her. She walks into her adjoining bedroom, pulls her thick cotton pajamas out of the top drawer of her bureau, and slips into them. Then she climbs onto her bed, on top of her striped comforter, and curls into the fetal position.

Meena has stopped crying. She feels like she has no

more tears left, like she's all dried up. But she knows that's not true. She knows tomorrow more tears will come.

Meena closes her eyes and tries to wipe all of the devastating images from her brain. She tries to remember her former life, when she was all smiles, full of motivation, and surrounded by friends. When one word from Justin lit up her day. When she won the blue ribbon at the Kennedy meet.

She curls her hand around the edge of the soft, worn comforter and thinks back even farther, to before Noah and Micah had ever left for college. When they'd taken her out for bike rides or taught her how to pitch a softball. When they'd all made pizza at home together. She remembers the weekend in middle school when her parents took them all to New York City to go to museums and learn more about Vietnam and to go shopping, see Broadway and the Empire State Building and the Statue of Liberty. She remembers how free and happy she felt, standing at the top of the statue, looking out at the world below.

Sooner than she expected, Meena starts to cry again. Because that Meena, that one in her former life, feels so very far away.

• • •

Tara clicks her tongue as Jeremy pulls his black Jetta into one of the spaces right in front of the TCBY in the Seneca Road strip mall. "We're too late," she says, craning her neck to look into the shop's floor-to-ceiling glass window. The lights are already dim. "They're closed."

Jeremy cuts the ignition and laughs at his girlfriend's

sad expression. She is never happy unless she satisfies her frozen yogurt fix. The girl could have a seven-course meal and she'd still need to finish it off with a helping of TCBY.

"Nah," Jeremy tells her. "I'm sure Reed left the door open."

Tara's dark eyebrows fly up. "You think?" she asks. But before Jeremy can even answer, she's already out of the car and on her way into the store, no doubt to secure her coffee-chocolate twist with rainbow sprinkles.

Jeremy locks the car and heads into the store himself. Just as he predicted, Reed is behind the counter. He's clearly in the middle of cleaning—he holds a mop in his hands—but he's asking Tara what she would like to have, anyway.

"Hey," Jeremy says, strolling inside and stepping up next to Tara. He rests his hand on the small of her back.

"Hey, Mandile," Reed says, slapping him five in greeting.

Jane Scott, Jeremy and Reed's classmate who often works the same shift as Reed, turns around from where she's Windexing one of the small tables in the corner of the narrow store. Her brown eyes widen, looking tired and vaguely annoyed behind her frameless glasses. "Reed, I thought you locked the door," she says.

Reed props the mop against the counter and rolls his eyes. "C'mon, Jane. It'll take two minutes," he says. He grabs a medium-size cup and places it under one of the yogurt machines.

"Hi, Jane," Jeremy says cheerily, hoping to snap her out of her obviously stressed state.

Her face relaxes a bit and she smirks. "Hi, Jeremy," she singsongs back. Then she smiles at Tara, but it's a little strained. These two just don't run in the same circles. "Sorry. I'm just kind of crazed."

"No problem," Jeremy says. He and Jane haven't exactly been friends for a long time. After middle school she went the honor society route while he went the not-so-stellar student athlete route. So he's not about to be offended by the fact that she's obviously hoping to rush him and Tara out the door. The girl is a well-known studyaholic and if she has a big old book to get back to, that's fine by him.

"It's just . . . I have to get out of here," Jane says with a sigh, looking at Reed. "And we haven't even cleaned the yogurt machines yet." She moves on to the next table, wiping with a vengeance.

"I'll take care of it." Reed glances over his shoulder at Jane as he tops off Tara's yogurt. "You're not gonna study more for AP French, are you?"

Jeremy notices that Reed actually looks concerned as he waits for Jane to respond. Jeremy finds this totally amusing—Reed is one of the biggest study dorks he knows. And one of the most competitive.

"No," Jane says. She moves back behind the counter, stuffing the Windex and the roll of paper towels onto a shelf. "I'm done with that, but I have to finish an extra-credit paper for history, I've got three articles going for the Web site, plus I have to finish a piece for music theory, practice my sax, and—"

"Okay! Okay, we get it!" Reed says with a laugh. He pulls out the big plastic container that holds the rainbow sprinkles, peels off the top, and rolls Tara's yogurt in it. "Don't worry about it. Go home. I'll close up." He hands the cup of yogurt to Tara. "On the house, as always," he says.

"Thanks," Tara responds, her brown eyes lighting up.

Jane unties the back of her apron and disappears into the back. She comes out a second later wearing a bulky blue backpack and headphones. "Thanks, Reed," she says. "See you guys tomorrow."

They all say their good-byes and Jane's about to walk right out when she stops and turns around. "You know, you guys are listed as Cutest Couple on Ears," Jane tells Jeremy and Tara, referring to the school's unofficial, gossipy Web site. "There's a great photo. You should check it out." Before they can ask Jane anything about it, she whips back around and is out the door.

"Cutest couple, huh?" Reed looks from Jeremy to Tara and shakes his head. "No shocker there."

"Hmmm," Tara says, biting down on her pink plastic spoon as she gives Jeremy a dimple-baring smile. "That's pretty cool, huh?"

"Yeah. It is." Jeremy fidgets with his gold pendant and tries to hide his own grin. He knows it's cheesy, but stuff like this makes him totally happy. Jeremy doesn't want to seem like a complete nerd, though. He knows he should play the whole thing down. "What's Jane doing reading Ears, anyway?" he asks Reed. "Doesn't she study, like, twenty-four seven?"

"Yup," Reed says. He picks up the mop and gets back to work cleaning. "That *is* work for her. She reads that rag to make sure Falls View isn't missing anything."

"You serious?" Jeremy asks, laughing. "That girl is unreal." Falls View is the school's *official* Web site, and Jane is the editor of it. "She even overstudies for her extracurriculars."

Reed stops mopping for a second to shoot Jeremy a look. "When she goes to Harvard, we'll see who's laughing."

Jeremy rolls his eyes. "I forgot who I was talking to."

Reed is one of those rare people who happens to be an *über*jock and an *über*brain. He spends a lot more time with Jane, in class and at work, than Jeremy does, and they are constantly up for the same academic awards. And even though he'd never admit it, Reed takes his studies very seriously. Although no one could take school quite as seriously as Jane Scott does.

Tara holds her yogurt in front of Jeremy. "Want some?"

"Sure. Thanks," Jeremy says. He grabs one of the little plastic spoons from the container on the counter and takes the cup from Tara, digging in.

Reed stops mopping for a second and glances at Jeremy. "Oh, sorry, man. Do you want anything?"

Jeremy hands Tara back her yogurt and notices that she's still smiling. He bends down and gives Tara a kiss on the top of her head, slinging his arm around her narrow shoulders.

"Thanks," Jeremy tells Reed. He gives Tara's shoulders a little squeeze. "But I don't need anything."

• • •

It's Sunday night, and Peter is lying in bed in his room.

Actually, it isn't really Peter's room. Up until a month ago this room was his parents' "office." What they really used it for, Peter has no clue, since neither of his parents ever brought their work home. How could they? His dad's a cop and his mom's a secretary, so their days both pretty much end when they leave the workplace.

Until recently the room was mostly filled with stacks of magazines—his father's *Time*s and *National Geographic*s and his mother's *Marie Claire*s and *Glamour*s. But after Peter had his accident, all of those magazines, along with the desk with the broken leg and the metal file cabinet, were brought down to the basement so that Peter could move in. His *real* bedroom is on the second floor, but since he can't use the stairs anymore, he was moved down here after the accident.

There's a light sequence of knocks on the door and Peter knows it's his mom. She always has to rap out a little song instead of just knocking like a normal person.

"Yeah. Come in," he says.

Peter's mom opens the door and steps inside, all smiles as usual. She walks over to Peter, tightening the belt on her pink terry cloth robe. "Just wanted to say good night," she says, perching herself on the edge of his bed.

Peter crosses his stocky arms across his chest. "Good night, Mom."

She leans in, holds one of her soft hands to his cheek, and kisses his other cheek. She smells way too floral. Peter knows it's that moisturizer she uses, the stuff his father buys her at Macy's for almost every occasion.

As his mom pulls away, she regards Peter for a moment. Her smile deepens. Her green eyes give off that same admiring vibe as they do when she coos over babies or puppies at the mall.

"You know, I was just speaking to your aunt Peggy," she says, clasping her hands in her lap. "She's so relieved that you're okay. And that you're getting better."

Peter blinks. *Well, that's just great. Good old Aunt Peg is relieved,* he thinks. This is the same woman who only recently started to talk to his mother again. For years she just couldn't accept that her dear little sister Laura had married and, *gasp,* had a child with a black man. And now Peter is supposed to care what she thinks?

"I'm not getting better, Mom," Peter says. "I don't know why you keep telling people that."

Her brow wrinkles and she folds her hands in her lap. "The doctors said it would take time—"

"Yeah, whatever," Peter interrupts. "Is that why you guys won't put in the chairlift thing on the stairs? Because you think I won't need it?"

"Peter, let's just wait and see," his mother says. "There's no reason to give up yet."

Right. No reason at all except that I haven't felt a thing below my waist since the night of the accident. The doctors said there was a chance he'd be able to walk again, but Peter almost wishes they never gave his parents hope.

Instead of dealing with reality, his mother and father seemed to take the doctors' words to mean he would be out of this chair in no time. In fact, they often act like Peter has simply come down with a temporary illness rather than undergone a life-altering spinal injury.

"I just want my room back," Peter says, aware that he sounds like a baby.

"What's wrong with this one?" his mother says, looking around the tiny room. "You have all your stuff."

Peter sighs audibly. He does have most of his things here—his bed, his desk, his old comic books. But there's one thing Peter can't stand about living down here in this tiny room off the kitchen: the lingering smell of stale cigarette smoke. This is where his mom used to come to have her daily nicotine fix.

Peter sits up, leaning his back against the wall. He does like the window he has here, though. It's big and it's right across from his bed, and it looks out onto part of the backyard and the neighbors' house several yards away. The window in Peter's room upstairs is tiny and not visible if you're lying in bed. Since bed is where Peter spends a lot of his time now—awake, though, not asleep—he appreciates having the view. But it doesn't exactly make all the negatives go away.

"Everything sucks," Peter says under his breath. Then he feels himself blush. He never tells his parents how he feels about everything. Not even in a vague way.

"Don't say that," his mother says quickly. "Everything is going to be okay."

That's what you believe, Peter thinks.

His mother shakes her head. She reaches out and touches Peter's arm, squeezing it lightly. "When I think about it—" She lets out an emotion-laden sigh, then lifts her hand and waves it in the air, as if to shoo away any ugly thoughts. "Well. We're just so lucky you made it through that accident okay."

But I'm not okay, Peter thinks. *Can't you see that?* But he resists the urge to yell. What would be the point?

"Yeah, Mom," he mumbles, scratching the back of his shaved head. This is only, like, the hundredth time his mother has said something to this effect. And it definitely doesn't make her statement any more true. Peter is not okay, and he feels anything but lucky.

Luck would be if that accident had killed him. Killed him good and young like he always imagined it would happen—as punishment. But someone had a much crueler sense of punishment. To make Peter live like *this*.

"Anyway. Get some sleep," his mother says, standing. She gives Peter a kiss on the top of his head and walks to the door. She turns when she reaches the doorway and asks, "Should I turn out the light?"

"Yeah. Go ahead," Peter says.

His mother flips the light switch and heads out, calling out, "Sleep tight," before she closes the door behind her.

Sleep tight. Yeah, sure. Peter lies all the way down. He hasn't slept tight in weeks. But he is tired. And there's no point in staying awake. So Peter shuts his eyes. Maybe he'll have a non-restless night for once.

But minutes after his eyes close, it's like his brain immediately opens. Opens and pours out all of the . . . crap. The
images from the accident, the nightmares that are always
lurking in his mind. All of it comes out at night.

Peter sees the blinding headlights heading straight for him,
hears the crunch of the car crashing into his door, hears the
crunch of his legs. Sees his legs—smashed up, trapped, and
bloody. Hears the sirens getting louder as they approach.

Peter tosses and turns. His heart races. He knows he
could just open his eyes and make it all disappear, but he
wants to sweat it out. Fight it. Relive these terrors and just
get on with it.

Peter lies in a stretcher on the road. He hears footsteps
charging toward him. But when the bodies attached to those
footsteps arrive, when those faces peer down at him, they are
not who he expects them to be—they are not the cops or the
doctors or Peter's friends. They are the faces of ten-year-olds.

Meena, Reed, Karyn, Jeremy, Jane, and Danny are all
staring down at him. Fear slides down Peter's body. What do
they want? Why are they haunting him? Then he sees that
they're not staring at him, exactly. They're staring at his hand.
At what's in his hand.

Peter opens his eyes, not able to take it anymore. He
doesn't want to see these visions. Doesn't want to face this fear.

He sits up, he's shaking, and he wants all of this to end.
He reaches to open the drawer in his nightstand and pulls
out a loose piece of gum. He hopes the chewing will calm
him down.

As Peter unwraps the gum and pops it in his mouth, he stares at the open drawer and thinks about that night. And how, because of what happened, he has to pay. He has to suffer. For the rest of his life.

Peter's heart slams against his chest as the next thought creeps into his brain.

Unless, of course, he cuts his life short.

CHAPTER FIVE

It's Monday and Meena sits in the corner of a classroom, her arms hugging her knees, which are pulled up to her chest. As Ms. Wayne, her homeroom teacher, reads off the morning announcements, Meena closes her eyes and tells herself she's going to be okay. She has to be. She has to keep on going. Pretend that nothing happened.

"Anyone interested in helping plan the winter formal should go to the social events meeting on Wednesday afternoon...," Ms. Wayne reads off her pink piece of paper.

Meena opens her eyes. It's hard to pretend when something *has* happened. When her world, her life, has been shattered. When her body feels heavy with anger and guilt and her skin burns with shame.

"Missy?" Ms. Wayne says. She steps back and leans on the edge of her desk at the front of the sunlit room. "You wanted to announce something?"

Meena drops her feet to the floor. Pulls her skinny shoulders up straight. She's still going to try to pretend, however. She has to. There's no other way.

Missy Hallestrom stands up from her seat in the front row and turns to face the homeroom. She flips her long blond hair behind her shoulder and smiles wide. "Just wanted to remind you all that we're playing East Meadow today in field hockey—and we're gonna kill 'em. So come on out and cheer us on!"

A couple of Meena's classmates clap and hoot as Missy sits back down, but all Meena can do is stare blankly ahead. None of this—this normalcy, this sanity—feels real. It all feels like a dream.

Meena knows that she used to share Missy's enthusiasm. She used to make spirit announcements in homeroom, too. But right now, that Meena seems like a completely different person. From another lifetime. And Missy Hallestrom's radiant smile, her bursting happiness, seem completely foreign to Meena. She knows she'll never feel that way again.

How can she when she still can feel remnants of his sweat on her skin? His gruff beard scraping against her cheek? When images of his greedy blue eyes, his greedy hands, keep flashing before her?

When she knows it could happen again? She's supposed to baby-sit on Wednesday.

I can't go back there, Meena thinks, staring down at the pseudogranite desktop. *I have to get out of it. Find someone else to do it. Or play sick.*

But whatever she does, it will only be a quick fix. She'll have to go back there again someday. She can't drop baby-sitting altogether or her parents will ask her why.

And it isn't like she can tell them. And when she doesn't have a good excuse, they'll tell her she has an obligation to the Claytons. A responsibility. They'll never let her break it.

Meena grabs her purple-and-black backpack up off the floor and clings onto it in her lap. Suddenly she feels the need to get out of here. To not be surrounded by people. Andy Souweine, a friend of Meena's, glances back at her from the second row and Meena's face heats up. She feels like he must know—like everyone must know. Like her shame is written across her face.

The bell ending homeroom rings and Meena jumps up without waiting for Ms. Wayne to dismiss them. She bolts out of the classroom and into the long hallway, which is not yet teeming with students. She just wants to get to her locker in the middle of the hall without running into any of her friends—she doesn't want them to see her face, look into her eyes. She doesn't want them to know.

Meena crosses her arms over her chest, hugging her jacket close to her as she makes her way toward locker number 103. Students start spilling out of classrooms now and Meena ducks her head, letting her long dark hair cover her face, hoping no one will see her.

She picks up her pace as she hears people laughing, singing, talking all around her. Their voices sound light and free and Meena feels heavy and trapped. She doesn't want to be anywhere near them.

Meena takes another step and bumps right into a skinny,

pale arm. She glances up briefly—the arm belongs to Danny Chaiken. He takes off his headphones and starts to say he's sorry, but Meena is already making her way around him.

Meena's almost at her locker when she sees Julia Nunez, a friend from the swim team, walking right toward her. "Some party at Luke's Saturday night, huh?" Julia says, cracking her gum as she talks.

Meena blinks. She can barely remember Saturday night. It feels like a year ago to her now. "Yeah," she says.

Julia seems to be looking at her funny—her large dark eyes are filled with confusion—and the shame rises up in Meena once again. Rises up and takes hold of her.

"See you later," Meena says quickly, then heads straight for her locker without looking back.

Meena takes her lock in her hands and starts to dial the combination. Her head is pounding and is crammed with memories of the nightmare that was last night. The smell of liquor on his breath, the scratching from his unshaven face, the pressing of his wedding band against her leg—

"Meen. You are never going to believe what Max Kang said in homeroom."

Meena slowly turns her head and sees Dana standing to the left of her. But Meena doesn't say anything. She can't. She's too wound up.

Dana frowns. She moves her backpack from one shoulder to the other. "Hello? You feeling okay?"

Meena shakes her head, as if to snap out of it. "Yeah.

Sorry. Just tired," she says, rubbing at her eyes. "I think I'm coming down with something."

"Oh. That sucks," Dana says. "Maybe it's all that drinking you did over the weekend."

"Yeah, maybe," Meena says distractedly. She catches a glimpse out of her peripheral vision of Jane Scott wheeling Peter Davis down the hall. It's weird, seeing Peter in a wheelchair. She's barely spoken two words to him since they were kids, but still . . . Meena briefly wonders what it would be like to be in a wheelchair, but it doesn't take her long to know that regardless, she would prefer it to living in her nightmare. She would gladly give up her legs in exchange for her freedom.

Dana glances at her watch. "Oops. Gotta go see Mr. Ward before class. I'll tell you about Max later." Dana turns. As she starts to walk away, she calls out, "Feel better."

Feel better. Meena hopes that's possible, but right now she can't see herself ever feeling better. She closes her eyes, takes a deep breath, and opens them. She looks at her lock and realizes that she was in a complete daze when she tried to open it a second ago. She probably didn't even dial the right combination.

Meena takes the lock in her hands again. She tells herself to just focus on opening the damn thing. That would be a start. Maybe if she just drowns out the terrors and goes about her day like normal, she'll actually start to feel normal again.

So Meena begins to dial. 9 . . . 14 . . . 34—

"Looking a little out of it today, Meen."

Meena jumps back as two strong hands grab her shoulders. She quickly turns around, her heart beating in her ears.

"Whoa. Sorry." Andy Souweine holds his hands up in the air. "I was just going to give you a little wake-up massage."

Meena's heart is still racing. She looks down at the floor, feeling stupid. Feeling horrible. "You scared me," she says.

"Apparently. Didn't mean to," Andy says. Meena's not looking at his face, but she can tell by the tone of his voice that he thinks she's lost it.

Well. He can just join the club.

"Anyway. See you later," she says, turning back around to face her locker.

"Oo-kay," Andy says.

Meena hears him walk away and she lets out a shaky breath. She once again grabs her lock, but when she tries to pull it open, the thing won't budge. She stares at the bright blue dial. The little white numbers start to blur as tears cloud her eyes.

And one thought runs through her brain: She will never feel normal again.

Ever.

• • •

Peter can think of only one thing as Jane Scott wheels him toward their African American literature class. He wants to yell at everyone to stop looking. Stop watching him. Because he can't take the stares, the furtive glances, or the sympathetic looks for one second longer.

86

It's Peter's second week back at school since the accident—he spent three weeks in the hospital and getting his strength back at home—and it's not getting any easier. In fact, this—this dealing with his classmates and their screwed-up reactions to seeing him in a wheelchair—is almost worse than not being able to walk. People are so ridiculously transparent.

Jane pushes Peter around a corner and he's greeted with a prime example of what he's thinking about. Some sophomore kid in an oversized sweatshirt practically stops in place when he glimpses Peter. The kid's eyes open wide and he just stands there, as if he's not even aware that he's staring. Finally the guy makes eye contact with Peter, turns bright red, and darts away like an idiot.

Now, that would fall into the first category—staring, Peter thinks. He wipes the palms of his hands against his brown pants and tries to focus straight ahead as Jane continues to push him down the hall. Even though Peter does his best to avoid looking at anyone as Jane wheels him, his neck muscles tense as he sees examples of all three categories of offensive looks. And the thoughts behind these looks are obvious.

First, there's the staring contingency. These are the people who register sheer shock when they encounter Peter. They're so stunned to see someone their age in a wheelchair, someone who was walking just like them so recently, that they can't even hide their reaction. Of course, once they snap to and realize that Peter has caught them looking at him, they immediately get embarrassed and look away.

Then there are the furtive glancers. These people think they're so careful, so sly, that Peter doesn't know they're regarding him like he's a freak show. But of course he knows. Right now, in fact, Peter can sense multiple sets of eyes, from all directions, bearing down on him. And Peter's certain they're all thinking the same thing: *Thank God that's not me.*

Jane pushes open the side door at the end of the hall that leads outside and wheels Peter down a shallow ramp. As the cool, fresh air hits his face, Peter is thankful that at least his handicapped status allows them to take this shortcut across a small expanse of grass over to the English hallway. At least he can escape his lame classmates and their looks if only for a brief moment.

Then, as if someone up above is trying to mock him or something, a girl walks toward him—who knows what the hell this chick's doing out here—and strikes Peter with the third and worst category—the sympathetic expression.

Peter doesn't even know this girl, but still, as she walks past him, hugging her books to her chest, she works hard to give Peter a caring look, to make her hazel eyes soften and convey the words, "I'm sorry." To show Peter that she feels bad about what's happened to him.

Don't! Peter wants to yell as the girl heads into the building he just came out of. *Don't pity me. You don't even know me.*

Peter swallows. He feels a knot in the pit of his stomach. That last look, the one of pity, gets to him the most. It's definitely the worst thing about being stuck in this wheelchair.

"Looks like it's going to rain."

Peter glances up at Jane, who's paused in front of the English wing to regard the gray cloudy sky. Being stuck with Jane definitely ranks up there in terms of what sucks about his situation. It's bad enough being forced to spend time with someone he used to be friends with but hasn't spoken to in years, but to put him at her mercy? That's just plain cruel. The situation couldn't be more awkward if Jane was an ex-girlfriend. Not that Peter *has* any ex-girlfriends, but still.

"Yeah," Peter says, once again wondering what the administration was thinking. On top of everything else, Jane Scott is the biggest goody-goody, straight-A overachiever in school. Peter and Jane have less than nothing in common.

Jane starts to push Peter again, this time up a narrow ramp, and it strikes him. *They were probably hoping she'd rub off on me*, he thinks. *That her psychotic study habits would make me less of a slacker.*

Well, that's definitely not going to happen. Jane's studying seems more pointless to Peter than ever.

Jane pushes open the door that leads to the English wing and Reed Fraiser—another sympathetic looker—grabs the door and holds it open so that Jane can wheel Peter into the hall.

"Thanks," Jane says to Reed.

"No problem," Reed says. But Peter doesn't look his way. He doesn't want to acknowledge Reed's pity-filled eyes, not even for a second.

Then, suddenly, images from last night's nightmare flash

89

into Peter's brain. With a chill, Peter remembers that both Jane and Reed were in that dream—as ten-year-olds. Ten. That was right when they all stopped hanging out together. Him, Reed, Jane, Jeremy, Meena, Karyn, and Danny. When everyone pretty much went their separate ways. Peter feels weird for a second. Unbalanced. Confused. But he shakes the eerie feelings off. After all, it was just a dream. Just his screwed-up mind playing tricks on him.

The hallway is crowded and a few junior guys are horsing around, tossing a football, but Jane manages to maneuver Peter toward the third door on the left, where their literature class is. She parks him right near the door, peers through its glass window, then shrugs off her backpack that looks like it weighs about a ton. She unzips the top, apparently searching for something.

The guys with the football come running in Peter's direction. One of them, Peter thinks his name is Bill or Bob, throws the football to the guy closest to Peter, a chubby dude named Evan. In his effort to catch the ball, Evan trips backward over a gym bag and before Peter can wheel himself out of the way, Evan falls smack-dab into Peter's lap.

"Hey! Watch it!" Jane shouts.

Peter's face immediately begins to burn. He feels like a helpless child, like an imbecile, with this big oaf stuck on top of him. The guy's greasy brown hair is centimeters from Peter's nose.

Evan quickly jumps up and proceeds to spout out a million apologies.

"Oh, man! I'm so sorry, I didn't see you there. I didn't—are you okay?"

Peter won't look at Evan. He can't. It will hurt what's left of his pride. "I'm fine," he mumbles.

But Evan's two idiot friends have to rush over, too. And Jane stands up. All of them are in Peter's face, asking him if he's all right. Talking to him as if he's a damn infant.

Didn't feel a thing! Peter wants to scream at them. *You could toss bricks on my legs and I'd be all right!*

But Peter doesn't say any of this. "I'm fine," he mutters. "Really." Peter grips his chair's armrests. He wishes he could make his face stop burning. The fact that he can't hide his humiliation makes him feel even more stupid.

"All right, guys, I think we're okay," Jane says firmly.

Thankfully, the Three Stooges take this as their cue and they back off. Evan, of course, has to let out one more "sorry" before he goes.

"Thanks," Peter says to Jane under his breath. He's not even sure she hears him, but she starts pushing again.

As Peter watches the guys head down the hall, as he watches his classmates stream past him to go into first period, that knot in his stomach twists and turns, ingesting his anger. His depression. Peter has always, always hated school, but now, in this chair, surrounded by these people, being here is more painfully miserable than ever.

Jane clears her throat. "So, did you do the essay for today?" Her voice sounds light, chirpy, and clearly forced. Like she's trying to snap Peter out of his bad mood.

Peter glares up at her. Is she for real? Does she really think Peter gives a crap about some English paper? "No. Didn't quite get around to it."

"Oh," Jane says. She pushes a couple of her springy curls away from her forehead and turns Peter's chair around in order to wheel him into their classroom. Peter doesn't bother to ask Jane if she wrote her essay. He doesn't care, and anyway, he knows the answer. She probably even wrote a second one for extra credit.

But as Jane pushes open the door—this time Diana Liu, a classmate and a furtive glancer, holds the door open as Jane wheels him inside—she mumbles, "Yeah. I didn't have time to write mine, either."

Peter looks up at Jane, surprised, as she wheels him over to the corner, toward the windows. "You didn't?" Peter asks. He really doesn't care, but still—Jane never doesn't do her homework. Or so he thought.

Jane nods. She bites at a thumbnail. Tension overtakes her childlike features. "I spent all last night working on a sax piece." She drops into the seat next to where she parked Peter and lets out a heavy sigh. "I wanted to speak to Ms. Alston before class to ask for an extension, but she's not even here yet."

Jane's black-stockinged leg begins to bounce up and down nervously and she continues to gnaw on her nails.

Peter can't help but smirk at Jane's little stress-out session. Ms. Alston comes rushing into class just as the bell rings and Jane looks like she's going to explode.

This is just perfect, Peter thinks. Here he is, sitting in a wheelchair with zero life ahead of him, while Jane worries if one late essay is going to mar her 4.0 average.

Peter shakes his head. Someone must have had a damn good laugh when they decided to pair them up. He just hopes they're having fun—because he sure as hell is not.

● ● ●

Meena trudges down the science wing in a daze, her hands pulled into the sleeves of her long-sleeved T-shirt. She weaves her way around clusters of students who are hanging out in the hall, talking, laughing, studying. Living their normal lives.

As she walks, Meena looks at no one and focuses on nothing. She tries to keep her brain blank. Empty. Because if Meena allows her mind to operate, to think, it immediately fills up with horrid flashes from last night—or floods with terrifying images of what might happen in the future. What might happen on Wednesday.

Chills run through Meena and she stops in place, wanting to cry all over again. How is she going to make it—through this day, this year, this life? How is she going to be able to go on?

Meena leans against a locker. Closes her eyes. *Forget,* Meena thinks. *Forget it ever happened.*

Meena opens her eyes. She lets out a deep breath so as to slow down her fast-beating heart. She takes her hands out from her sleeves and glances at her watch. 1:02. Only two more periods left. And then swim practice.

You can do this, she tells herself, her fingers clutching the cuffs of her shirt. *You can make it through the day.*

So Meena moves away from the locker and begins to walk again. She trips over someone's outstretched legs, but she barely notices. Barely hears the person say they're sorry. Meena's in a daze. That's the only way she's going to be able to function.

"Meena! I've been looking for you."

Meena turns her head to the right, to the source of the voice, which belongs to Jane Scott. Jane is holding on to the back of Peter Davis's wheelchair and both of them—both Jane and Peter—are looking at Meena with a startled expression. Once again Meena thinks the only thing she can think: *They know.* She crosses her arms over her chest. To protect herself. To hide.

"Stay right there. I'll be right back." Jane says, and Meena simply nods. She feels heavy and drained and she doesn't want to move, anyway.

Meena watches as Jane wheels Peter into room 304, wondering for the second time today what Peter is feeling, being in that wheelchair.

Jane comes darting back out of the classroom and walks right up to Meena. She tugs at the collar of her white blouse as if it's irritating her neck. "I need your piece," Jane says. When Meena doesn't respond, Jane prods, "The profile on Reed Frasier for the sports page? Do you have it?"

Meena shakes her head. The piece—the article for the Falls View—is the last thing on her mind. Meena has not written it yet, and she can't imagine doing it anytime in the future. In fact, she can't see ever going to a Falls View meeting again. How can she when it requires all of her energy just to walk through the hall?

Jane's dark eyes bug open wide. Her eyebrows shoot up. She looks like she's going to combust. "Meena! That was due last week. I really need it! Mr. Bonnebaker's going to kill me if we're under on stories again."

Meena doesn't know what to say. So she lies. "Sorry. I'll give it to you at the meeting eighth period," she mumbles.

"All right," Jane says. "Sorry, I don't mean to be so uptight. I just want to get it done, okay?"

Meena can't stand to look into Jane's honest eyes one second longer, so she stares at the green-and-blue pattern of Jane's plaid skirt. "Okay," she says.

"Meena, I—" Jane begins to say, her tone still apologetic, but is interrupted by the ringing of the bell. Jane glances at her watch, curses under her breath, and says, "I'll see you later." She rushes away, heading to her next class.

Meena just stands there, watching Jane book down the hall and around the corner, watching the swarms of students rush past her, rush around her. She feels sick. And tired. And dead.

The thought of sitting through two more classes, of being tormented by her thoughts while everyone stares at her, knowing that something's very wrong, now seems undoable to Meena. It seems impossible.

Meena clutches the straps of her backpack and doesn't give it a second thought.

She runs. Past the classrooms, past her classmates, past the school lobby. She runs right out the door, down the stairs, and makes a mad dash for her car at the far end of the parking lot, barely even feeling the drops of rain that sprinkle down on her.

When Meena gets to her Honda, she's out of breath and sweating and she fumbles to find her keys in the front pocket of her backpack.

But when Meena does grab her keys and unlocks her door, she's relieved. Because maybe if she drives the hell out of here, if she goes somewhere and blares music, inhales some smoke, maybe even chugs down some alcohol, maybe then she can make it through the rest of the day.

Maybe.

CHAPTER SIX

The following day, after school at swim practice, Meena is the last girl out of the locker room.

Meena never used to be last. She always used to be first—first one in the water, first to psych the rest of the team up, first in place. First to laugh.

Meena also never used to get stoned. But that's exactly what she is as she pushes open the swinging locker-room door and steps into the narrow, tiled hallway that leads to the pool.

Today was just as torturous as yesterday, but Meena did manage to make it through all of her classes. She has her brother's pot to thank for that. Last night Meena was rifling through Noah's desk drawer to look for a pack of cigarettes when she came across a baggie with some weed in it and a small brass pipe. Desperate to find a way to quiet her screaming brain, to dull her cutting emotions, Meena grabbed the pot and smoked it before she went to bed. This morning she didn't know how she could come back here and endure a whole day of classes. So she smoked again before school and during her free last period, in the parking lot of the 7-Eleven, so she could get herself to swim practice. But suddenly the pot doesn't seem like enough.

Meena wraps her arms around herself as she walks to the end of the hallway. She feels uncomfortable in her navy blue Speedo and she keeps pulling down on it, wishing it would cover her more. The bathing suit never used to bother her, but now she resents the way it clings to her body. That it reveals so much. She hates the fact that Steven came to a meet a couple of weeks ago—the same one Justin came to. She hates that Steven's seen her in this suit.

Meena feels like she's moving in slow motion as she pushes open the glass door that leads to the pool area. The door feels much heavier than usual—Meena has to push hard—and for a brief moment she wonders if she is really awake and at school right now or if this is all just a dream.

But once Meena manages to get the door open and the cloudy chlorine smell invades her nostrils, she knows that she's awake. She's here.

"Meena, where were you yesterday?"

Meena glances over at Coach Krakauer. The coach is looking at Meena with a confused expression, but Meena is used to this by now. And because she's high as a kite, because she's smoked so much pot, she might as well be a zombie, she doesn't care. Meena doesn't even care that as she walks to the foot of the pool, all of her teammates who are gathered on the wooden benches facing Coach are looking at her like she's nuts.

Meena feels her ears start to burn and she amends that last thought: Maybe she does still care. Just not as much.

"I had an appointment," Meena lies to Coach Krakauer, stepping up next to her. The coach is tall and she towers over Meena.

Coach Krakauer shakes her head. Worry lines pop up at the corners of her mouth. But she takes her steady gaze off Meena for a moment to address the rest of the team. "Start lining up at the pool. We'll begin in a second."

Meena's teammates all stand up and move around, heading for the other end of the pool. Meena can feel them shuffling around her, she can feel them looking at her, and once again she is thankful for the pot, which still gives her a certain carefree lightness.

"You should have dropped off a note," Coach says, her full attention now focused on Meena. She seems to be trying really hard to look right into Meena's eyes and it's bugging Meena out. Sending her neurons into alert mode and causing a queasiness to overtake her body. "Or at least told someone else on the team. I had no idea where you were. And this is the third time you've missed practice in the past few weeks."

Meena looks down to the ground. She focuses on the dirt trapped in the grooves of the white tiles. "Sorry," she says. She had skipped a couple of times to get to the Claytons' early. To hang out with Steven. The thought only intensifies her queasiness.

Coach lets out a frustrated-sounding sigh. "Yes. Me too." She makes no attempt to hide the anger in her tone. "We'll talk about this more later. Why don't you just get to the front of one of those lines and start off with a front crawl? You'll swim extra laps today to make up for yesterday."

Meena doesn't say anything. She just nods. And walks away from Coach Krakauer, toward the pool. And her teammates. Who are all staring at her.

Meena heads along the right side of the pool, the side next to the wall of windows. But now, as she walks, she doesn't feel light and airy anymore. She feels heavy and off balance. Like it requires a lot of work to take each step. And she has to be careful, or she might trip.

And suddenly she does care, she *really* cares, that everyone's eyes are on her. She wonders what they are thinking. She wonders if they've figured it out. If they know.

Meena reaches the head of the pool, where everyone else is formed into four neat lines.

"Carrie, let Meena jump ahead of you," Coach Krakauer calls out from the other end.

Carrie Willner takes a step back and Meena tries very hard not to look at anyone as she takes her place at the head. She stares down at the still, greenish blue water, and all of a sudden she can't wait to dive in. To dive in and swim away—from their stares, from her fears, from her life.

Meena lowers her goggles down over her eyes and crouches into starting position. She immediately loses her balance, almost falling in. But she recovers quickly enough, crouches down again, and stares down at the inviting water.

Coach blows her whistle and Meena dives in. She welcomes the way the water envelops her body, the comforting familiarity of swimming in the pool.

But after Meena completes a couple of strokes, she begins to feel disoriented. Like she can't quite get her legs and arms to move the way that they should. Her limbs feel thick, and slow, and uncoordinated. Like they're not necessarily connected to her body.

And Meena's goggles suddenly feel like they're on too tight, as if they're cutting off the circulation to her brain. She feels like she's losing her breath, and she has to stop swimming for a moment, lift her head from the water, and gulp some air. She then ducks her face back into the water and continues with her front crawl, but she still feels completely off. Like she's battling just to swim in a straight line.

Meena's left hand finally hits the edge of the pool and she stops swimming, letting her feet touch the bottom. As she pulls herself up and out of the water, she notes the silence. The lack of talking. She glances over her shoulder and sees that the three other girls who dove into the pool when she did have already climbed out and walked back to the head of the diving blocks.

Everyone is waiting for Meena. Watching her.

Meena quickly whips her head back around as she stands all the way up. Her knees feel like they might give in. She knows she was swimming slowly, but not *that* slowly. . . .

"What was that?"

Coach Krakauer is walking up to Meena and she looks mad. Pissed.

The weird thing is, Meena doesn't really care. Swimming used to be one of the things Meena cared about most, what she focused so much attention on, but now it doesn't even seem to matter. Meena's desire to kick butt on the swim team is just another item on the long list of things that feel like they belong to another lifetime.

So Meena simply stands there, water dripping off her, and shrugs. "I don't know."

Coach's light eyebrows fly up. Her mouth sets into a straight line. She hugs her clipboard to her chest and shakes her head. "You don't know?" she repeats. "Well, you better figure it out."

Meena has no idea what to say, so she just stares down at the ground again.

"Meena, if you don't get your act together, you're not going to be able to stay on the team."

Meena nods. She already knows this. She already knows that there's no way she can stay on this team. She doesn't have the energy. All she'll do is disappoint everyone. And make them wonder. Meena's stomach twists and turns. What if she makes them wonder so much that they start to ask questions?

Meena glances up at the Coach. "I know," she says. "And I quit."

Once again Meena finds herself surrounded by deafening silence. Coach goes pale, obviously shocked. But Meena has nothing more to say. She just wants to get out of here. So she starts to walk away, into the hall that leads to the locker room.

"Next in line, dive in. I'll be back in a second," Meena hears Coach call out. Then she hears the coach's running footsteps behind her.

"Meena. Wait a minute."

Meena stops in place. Turns around.

Coach Krakauer drops her clipboard at her side. Her deep-set eyes soften. "Are you okay?"

Meena shrugs. "Yeah. Just tired."

Coach walks up closer to her. She rests a hand on Meena's shoulder and peers searchingly into her face. "I know you've missed a few practices lately and I came down kind of hard back there, but you don't have to quit the team. I know how much you love swimming, Meena. Don't make a snap decision you'll regret."

I'm doing all kinds of things that I'll regret, Meena thinks, feeling utterly pathetic.

Drawing her hand away, Coach crosses her arms over her chest, hugging her clipboard to her. "What's going on with you, Meena? You were so off in the pool and I've never seen you be this quiet before. You don't seem like yourself."

Meena stares back at the coach. *That's because I'm not me,* she thinks. *That me is gone.* "I'm burned out on swimming, I guess."

"Really?" Coach Krakauer asks. "It's not something else? Everything's all right at home?"

Meena nods, swallowing as she does so, but the coach keeps her eyes carefully trained on her, as if she doesn't believe her.

"Well, all right." Coach Krakauer glances back in the direction of the pool, clearly feeling the obligation to get back in there. She looks back to Meena, taking a step away. "But if you decide tomorrow that you want back on the team, just come see me. We'll work something out."

"Okay," Meena says. She turns toward the locker room, wanting to escape.

"Meena? Will you promise me one thing?" Coach Krakauer says.

Meena pauses. Takes her hand off the locker-room door.

"You'll go see your guidance counselor? Explain things to her? Tell her why you're feeling burned out?" Coach says. "That's what she's there for."

"Yeah. Sure," Meena responds, even though she has no intention of doing so. And before Coach can ask any more questions, dole out any more suggestions, Meena pushes open the door and heads inside the locker room.

She grabs a towel from the big stack to the right of the door and wraps it around her like a blanket. She walks over and sits down on the bench in front of her locker.

Her guidance counselor is Ms. Aufiero—Karyn's mother. There's no way Meena could ever tell her anything. What if she did and then Ms. Aufiero told Karyn? Or her parents? Meena wraps the towel more tightly around her, chills running up and down her arms.

What if Meena told Ms. Aufiero, told her everything, and then Ms. Aufiero confirmed what Meena already knows? That everything that Steven has done to her is her fault?

Meena's eyes blur with tears and she stands up. She needs to get dressed, get out of here, and get high again.

The numbness is starting to wear off.

• • •

"Did you see the size of her hickey?" Nick Scopetta asks Danny and Cori as they linger outside their drama classroom at the end of the day. "Who the hell would kiss *her*?"

Danny rips open the small bag of Doritos that he just got out of the vending machine and pops a couple of chips in his mouth. The "her" that he, Nick, and Cori are currently in the process of ripping apart is Erica Ebner, a stick-up-her-butt princess who thinks she's the best actress in the school. She blew up at Danny at the end of the class, yelling at him that he was making her lose her concentration with his "idiotic jokes."

But Danny couldn't care less. He's in a great mood, and not even Erica can bring him down. He loves when this happens—when his energy soars for no particular reason. He just hopes it will last. "She probably got her dog to suck on her neck," Danny says.

Cori and Nick both laugh. Danny smiles at his own joke, popping a few more chips into his mouth. He's having such a good time hanging out with these two, he feels like he could chill in this hallway forever, he feels like—

"Oh! I gotta go," Cori says, glancing down at her Wonder Woman watch. "I gotta get to work."

Danny glances down at his own watch and his stomach turns over as he realizes that he has to go, too. Today is

Tuesday. That means his mother will be waiting for him in the parking lot. Waiting to drive him to Dr. Lansky's for his weekly shrink appointment.

Suddenly Danny feels like punching something. Erica Ebner might not be capable of ruining his happy spirits, but that annoying shrink sure is.

Cori scoops her camouflage backpack up off the floor. "You guys coming?" she asks.

"Yeah. I am," Nick says.

Danny reluctantly picks up his own backpack, his good mood almost completely evaporated. "Me too," he says with a sigh. Oh, well, obviously that good mood swing isn't going to last after all.

Cori and Nick both turn, heading for the stairwell at the end of the hall. Danny trudges slowly behind them, angry, annoyed thoughts zigzagging through his brain.

I don't even want to go to the stupid shrink, Danny thinks, gripping his backpack straps as he begins to walk down the stairs. Actually, the worst part about this is not the fact that Danny has to go to the doctor, although that does suck. The worst part is that his mother insists on driving him to his appointments because she doesn't trust that he'll go on his own. She thinks he'll ditch. Usually he drives his own car to school, but on days when he has to see the shrink, his mom drops him off in the morning—a few blocks from school so no one will see—and picks him up afterward.

When Danny gets to the landing, he stops for a moment.

"You guys go ahead," he calls to his friends. "I forgot something in my locker."

"Okay," Cori calls back, reaching the door that leads to the lobby. "Bye."

"Later, Chaiken. See you tomorrow," Nick says.

"Tomorrow," Danny responds, waving as Nick and Cori head into the lobby.

Danny watches the heavy metal door slam behind them. But he doesn't move. Because he didn't leave anything in his locker. He just wanted his friends to go ahead so that they wouldn't have to see him getting picked up by his mommy.

As he waits, Danny empties the remains of his Doritos bag into his mouth, then crumples up the bag and tosses it in the garbage. Okay, so fine. Danny did skip a few appointments in the beginning. But he promised he'd never do it again. He swore. Why don't his parents believe him? Why do they insist on driving him around like he's the same age as his little sisters?

No, Danny decides suddenly. *Wait a minute.* He shouldn't let this Lansky creep, or his parents, ruin his superlative mood. He slips his backpack off his skinny shoulders, grabs his Discman out of his front pouch, and puts his headphones on, blasting his Tool CD.

Screw them, he thinks, heading for the swinging door and bopping his head to the music. He'll just deal, get in the car, and sit through the stupid appointment. He doesn't have to talk to the doctor or even listen to him if he doesn't want to.

Yeah. That's it, Danny decides, stepping into the lobby. He'll make the best of the situation. He won't let everyone else get him down.

Still, when Danny walks through the school entrance and immediately spots his mother's station wagon idling at the bottom of the steps, annoyance surges through him all over again.

Just chill, Danny tells himself. *Just get into the music.*

Danny closes his eyes for a second, turns up the volume on his Discman, then jogs down to meet his mom, opening the door and sliding into the passenger seat. "Hey, Mom," he says.

"Danny!" his mother exclaims, her blue eyes opening wide. "That music is so loud. *I* can hear it."

"Sorry," Danny says as his mother shifts into drive. He turns the volume down a bit, then lets out a short laugh. "I thought chauffeurs were supposed to let their passengers do whatever they want, though."

His mother turns to give him a look as she drives out of the parking lot. It's a look that Danny has seen many times before, one that says, *I'm way too tired—of you. Stop trying my patience.*

"Sorry," Danny says, rolling his eyes. "It was a joke."

"Well, considering I've been waiting for you for fifteen minutes, I guess I'm not really in a joking mood," his mom retorts. "You're going to be at least five minutes late as it is."

Danny fidgets with the door lock. "Wow. Five whole minutes. Call the police," he quips.

His mom gives him another one of her patented looks, this time managing to relay all of her annoyance just out of the corner of her eye. Danny sulks, but he shuts up. He doesn't feel like fighting. So he won't talk anymore. He'll just look out the window, listen to his music, and mind his own business.

That's the plan, at least. But as his mother turns onto Oak Drive, Danny starts to feel kind of funny. Unsettled. His stomach is churning, and a Dorito aftertaste begins to crawl up the sides of his throat.

Danny rips off his headphones. He feels like he's going to be sick.

He grips the edge of his upholstered seat cushion, pursing his lips and trying to eliminate the dryness that's spreading through his mouth. Come to think of it, he's felt a little queasy all day. But now it's hitting him with full force.

"Mom, I think your driving is making me sick," Danny jokes as his mom brakes at a red light.

His mom sighs. Pushes some of her dyed blond hair behind her ear. "Very funny."

Danny pales. He grips the seat tighter. "No, really. I'm not kidding. I feel totally nauseous."

His mother turns to look at him, her eyebrows knitting together. For a brief moment she no longer looks annoyed. She actually appears concerned. "It's your stomach?"

A car behind them honks and his mom looks straight ahead. Seeing the light has turned green, she steps on the gas.

"Yeah," Danny says, the queasiness spreading. He feels

dizzy. Weak. Green. "My stomach is totally screwed up. I don't think I can sit through my appointment."

His mother's shoulders slump. "Danny." She shakes her head. "I'm not going to fall for this," she says. "We can't go through this every week. You're not missing your appointment."

Danny can't believe his mom thinks he's faking it. Okay, fine, so he did fake a headache that one time, but still. He feels really damn nauseous! Like he's going to throw up. "Mom, I'm serious," he says through clenched teeth. "I'm sick. I think it's from the medication."

"Now it's the medication that's making you sick?" his mom challenges. Her voice sounds tired. Irritated. "It's not all the junk food you eat?"

"No!" Danny exclaims. Why won't she just believe him? "'Cause I've always eaten junk food, always, my whole life, and I never get sick. Not like this." A bubble of that Dorito taste rises up again. He begins to sweat.

His mother turns into Lansky's parking lot and the jerking movement makes Danny even more queasy. More sick to his stomach.

"Okay," his mother says, pulling into a spot. "You can talk about all of this with Dr. Lansky. He'll tell you if it's the medication. But you are not missing this appointment."

Danny's mom shifts the car into park and turns to look at him, as if to say that she's waiting for him to get out and get in there already.

Danny curses under his breath and pops open his door.

And as he does so, an uncontrollable wave, an all-consuming nausea, overtakes him and he can't take it any longer.

So Danny does what he needs to do. He looks down at the asphalt, which is all blurry and fuzzy, and he lets it out. He pukes. In one satisfying release.

Danny hates to throw up, but the minute all of the bile, all of the acid, is out of his stomach, he feels instantly better. A new man.

Still, his mom doesn't need to know that.

Danny slowly lifts his head, wipes at his damp face. He looks to his mom and sees that she has a hand on her mouth and her forehead is crinkled in concern. Her eyes are apologetic.

Danny is glad that she's sorry. She deserves to be.

"There," he says, crossing his arms over his chest. "*Now* can we go?"

• • •

As Meena steps into the spacious school lobby that afternoon, she feels like she can't get to her car soon enough. The effects of the pot have worn off, the good ones at least, and now she just feels tired, drained, and flipped out.

She trudges through the wide entrance, gripping the straps of her backpack as she walks outside. All Meena wants to do is go home, bury herself in her bed, and sleep. Forever.

But as Meena begins to slump down the front steps, she sees a familiar face heading her way from the parking lot. A face that for a brief moment pulls Meena out of her miserable haze.

"Meena!" Holly Finneran calls out.

As Meena watches Holly pick up her pace, hurrying to meet her on the steps, she feels a rush of warmth, a rush of comfort, wash over her. Holly is one of Meena's closest friends—they've been tight ever since they met when they were in grade school. But Holly is a year older than Meena and now she's in college. She hasn't gone very far, just fifteen minutes away to Skidmore College in Saratoga Springs, where both Holly and Meena's moms are professors. But considering how wrapped up Holly is in her new life at school, how little she and Meena now talk, Meena sometimes thinks that Holly might as well be in California.

Still, when Holly rushes up to Meena and gives her a big hug, Meena feels like no time has passed between them.

"It's so good to see you!" Holly says as she pulls away.

"Yeah. You too," Meena responds. As she regards her friend, takes in Holly's small blue eyes that are overflowing with enthusiasm, sees that she still wears that little pearl on a gold chain around her neck, Meena is immediately brought back to happier times. When she and Holly would play harmless pranks on other members of the swim team. When they'd go for long bike rides through the falls. When they'd laugh for hours. When things were easier.

Meena fidgets with her thumb ring, her stomach turning over. When Meena's life wasn't a nightmare.

Holly glances down at her gold-and-silver watch, then

looks back up at Meena. "Practice isn't over, is it? I came by to watch you guys."

Meena shakes her head. She slips her backpack off her shoulders and drops it at her feet. "They're still in there. I took off early."

"Why?" Holly asks. She pulls the hair elastic out of her ponytail, and her straight brown hair falls to her shoulders. "You're not feeling well?"

"No," Meena says. She's about to lie to Holly, to tell her she hasn't been sleeping or that she's coming down with something like she's been telling everyone else, but then, because this is Holly, because this is the one person Meena used to tell everything to, something happens that Meena can't control: Tears spring to her eyes.

"Meen, what's wrong?" Holly asks, stepping closer to her.

Meena shakes her head as a couple of tears fall down her cheeks. She holds up a hand to wave Holly off, to say that she's really fine, but she can't stop the tears from flowing. So she drops down on the step, trying to dry her eyes with her fists.

Holly sits down next to Meena. She rubs her back. "What's going on?" Holly asks. "I'm sorry I've been so busy. I've been meaning to call you, it's just with classes and swimming and everything, I'm barely in my room."

"It's okay. It's not that," Meena says. She sniffles. Take her hands away from her eyes. And as Meena looks at Holly, the weirdest thing happens. She almost feels like she

113

can tell Holly. For the first time since Sunday night, she almost feels like she can actually open her mouth and let the words come out. Almost.

"Well, what is it, then?" Holly asks. She rests her pointed chin in the palm of her hand and watches Meena patiently. Meena knows that Holly would sit with her here for hours if she asked her to.

Meena hugs her legs to her chest. She gazes out at the sprinkling of cars that remain in the vast parking lot. Maybe she *can* tell Holly. After all, Holly does understand Meena better than anyone else. Maybe there is a way out of this hell that Meena has been trapped in.

She glances back at Holly and her stomach drops at the mere thought of uttering the words aloud. Saying it out loud would make it so real. And then she'd have to deal with it. Do something. And Meena's not sure she's up to that. She rubs at her eyes again, lets out a heavy breath, and stares down at her sneakers. It's a terrifying thought, telling Holly—just the idea of it makes Meena's skin prickle and itch—but it would also be a relief to release what's been gnawing away at her. It would be *such* a release—if Meena could be sure that Holly wouldn't judge her. Wouldn't be disgusted. Wouldn't think *she* was a monster.

She takes a deep breath. Tries to start slowly.

"I've been baby-sitting for the Claytons a lot," Meena says. Her cheeks immediately flush. She barely knows how those words made their way out of her mouth.

"Really?" Holly says, taking in Meena's blushing face.

For a split second Meena thinks Holly's figured it out and Meena won't even have to say it. It must be written all over her face.

"Omigod! You still totally lust after Steven Clayton, don't you?" Holly says, grinning.

Holly's words cut right into Meena. *Still . . . totally . . . lust . . .*

Holly flips her hair to one side. "Mmm. Steven Clayton. I see him around campus, you know. Still looking good. Remember how we used to stare at that photo of him at your house? The one where he's at the beach in Mexico with your dad?"

Meena's insides are being torn to shreds, along with any hope that she can reveal the truth. Her eyes quickly dart back to her sneakers; the tears threaten to resurface. "Yeah," Meena says quietly.

"So? Is that what's bothering you?" Holly asks. "Your unrequited love?"

Meena feels like she's been kicked in the stomach, like she can't breathe. She feels shaky—like she might collapse at any moment.

She already knew this. Already knew that she'd always had a crush on Steven Clayton. But hearing Holly say it makes it all the more real. Guilt and self-blame overtake Meena's brain; they greedily occupy every ounce of space in her mind and in her heart, not leaving room for anything else.

All she can do is hate herself.

Meena stands on weak legs. Grabs her backpack. "You know what? I think I gotta go home," she says.

Holly bolts up. "You sure? I just got here."

Meena nods. She shoulders her bag and tells herself to move quickly before she starts to cry again. "I have a headache. I'm a mess today. You wanted to see the rest of the team, anyway."

"Okay," Holly relents. "But I'm gonna call you soon." She pulls Meena into another quick hug and it takes all of Meena's restraint to not just break down in Holly's arms. "Feel better."

Unable to speak—if Meena opens her mouth, she knows nothing but sobs will come out—Meena simply nods again, then turns around and makes a beeline for her car. She has to just go home. And hide in bed.

There is no way out.

CHAPTER SEVEN

It's Wednesday. Last period. Meena sits in the back corner of her history elective, frozen. This is what she's been like all day, just awake enough to walk, talk a little bit, and generally do a feeble impersonation of a normal person.

But Meena tries very hard not to be awake enough to feel. Or think. Because then her pain and her fear overcome her. Trap her. She thinks about having to go over to the Claytons' tonight, of what will happen if Steven catches her alone. . . .

Meena's attempts at not letting her brain roam and meander are futile. Even as she sits here now, her eyes blurring on the middle space, the sound of Mr. Roosevelt lecturing filling up her ears, she can't prevent Steven from entering her mind and poisoning her thoughts.

Steven is the only image that will present itself in Meena's imagination. Steven's leering blue eyes, Steven's clammy hands, Steven's forceful lips.

Meena's grip tightens on her pen. Her pulse races and her mouth dries out as another helping of fear travels down her spine. She tries to make herself forget, tries to bury it all, but she is punished instead with a tactile memory of the way his lips felt against her bare skin.

Meena's heart jumps and she drops her pen. She watches it roll across the linoleum floor, too far for her to reach. A couple of her classmates seem to notice, but none of them are close enough to the pen to pick it up for her. Meena herself is too tired to even think about getting up out of her seat.

She looks at the blackboard, where Mr. Roosevelt is now writing down dates—dates that must relate to his lecture somehow—and Meena resolves that she's going to try to focus on class. Take notes. Drive all of this other crap right out of her brain.

So Meena reaches down and digs into the front pouch of her backpack to look for another pen. She finds a pencil, and when she pulls it out, a little scrap of paper comes flying out as well. It's white and it looks like a ticket stub. Meena scoops it up and places it on top of her open notebook.

It's the stub from the Dave Matthews concert that she and her friends went to back in April.

Meena turns the ticket over in her hands, fingers its jagged edge. She desperately wants to think of something happy, of something nonscary, and now the opportunity presents itself. Meena sits back in her chair and lets the memory come flooding back.

It was a warm night, unseasonably so for April. Meena had felt high on life as she danced with Dana, Luke, Reed,

Karyn, and Karyn's boyfriend, T. J., at the outdoor concert space in Saratoga, under the light of a full moon. They were all enjoying the good vibes the crowd was giving off—everyone seemed psyched to be there, just like Meena was. She and Luke got silly, started ballroom dancing to one of the slow songs—twirling each other jokingly as all their friends laughed and ducked their heads from embarrassment.

Meena feels a smile tugging at the corners of her lips as she sits in class and remembers that night. Remembers how much fun she had with Luke that evening. That was how they used to be together—total hams, cutups, shoo-ins for the class clown vote. When Luke had dipped her at the end of their dance, they lost their balance and fell to the ground, Luke right on top of Meena, and all their friends laughed and teased them. "Kiss her! Kiss her!"

Then, just as Meena is remembering Luke's serious blush at that moment, she stiffens. Her hands grasp the edge of the desk attached to her chair. Just as she was remembering that moment, just as she was thinking about one of her favorite times ever, Luke's face morphed into Steven's. His warm blue eyes turned into Steven's cold, hard ones, his awkward, playful touch into Steven's forceful one.

Meena grabs the ticket stub and rips it in half, disgust and anger rushing through her. Not even her memories—her happy ones—are safe for her anymore. Steven has ruined them.

The bell rings and Meena stands immediately, grabbing her bag. She has no idea where she's going to go now that school's over, but she knows that she has to go somewhere. Somewhere she can escape the thought of Steven. Somewhere she can be alone and try to figure out a way to get out of seeing him tonight.

A way out of seeing him ever again.

• • •

If one more waitress bumps into the back of Peter's wheelchair, then follows it up with a horrified apology, Peter is going to lose it.

It's after school and Peter's chair is pulled up to a small booth at the Falls Diner, a popular hangout for Falls students since it's only a couple of blocks from school.

Peter can usually spend hours here just goofing off and drinking coffee, but now that he's stuck in this wheelchair, now that it's too much of a pain to slide into one of the brown fake leather booths like every other person in the restaurant is capable of doing, he feels totally on edge. Like he can't stay here much longer.

Of course Max, Keith, and Doug, comfortably nestled into opposite sides of the booth, are oblivious to Peter's annoyance. Max is chomping down on onion rings, he and Doug laughing as Keith relates the funnier moments of a Howard Stern interview he caught on cable late last night. It's the first time Doug has actually come out with the rest of them since Peter's accident, and he's still not really speaking directly to Peter.

"I mean, no matter what she said to him, he would not stop asking her if her boobs were real. She got all mad and stormed out and he ripped on her for like ten minutes! It was so funny, I practically pissed myself," Keith says, grabbing one of the onion rings and popping it into his mouth. "I mean, what do you expect when you go on *Stern*? A serious discussion about world peace?"

Peter's chair jolts forward a bit, the wheels bumping into the base of the table.

"Oh! I'm sorry, sweetheart," says Norma, a big hulking waitress who's probably been working at the diner since the early seventies.

Peter nods, not bothering to look up at her. He can't take another pity glance and besides, those drawn-on eyebrows of hers freak him out. "It's okay."

"Have any of you ever seen the show where Beetlejuice and Stuttering John wrestle?" Max asks.

Peter shakes his head no, but Keith says, "Yes! That's the best ever, dude!" He scoots to the edge of his seat, as if he needs to get closer to Max to discuss Howard Stern's humor, and Peter zones out. They've only had this conversation, like, three hundred times before.

Slurping down some of his Coke, Peter glances around the too bright diner to keep himself occupied. This place is the ideal people-watching spot, and Peter has amused himself plenty of times by watching idiot jocks get into a fight or overhearing some of the princessy popular girls gossip wickedly about their supposed friends.

But as Peter looks around today, the scene seems fairly tame. There's a cheesy-looking sophomore couple sharing a sundae in the corner booth, some geeky freshmen study-ing in the next booth over . . . then Peter's eyes rest on Meena Miller, who slumps in the next booth, by herself, smoking a cigarette.

As he watches her light another cigarette off the butt she's smoking, then put the stub out in an already filled ashtray, he immediately has a flash of the nightmare from the other night. The one where he saw Meena, and the others, when they were ten years old.

Peter wraps his hands around his cold soda glass, over-come by a strange tingle of foreboding that runs down his back. He hasn't thought about Meena for years, and then, bam, he has a nightmare with her in it? He noticed her in school Monday, when Jane was bugging her about some-thing, and now here she is again. Peter rubs his cool, damp hands against the legs of his black pants, still watching her. Okay, so it's not so weird that he keeps seeing Meena. He does go to school with the girl. But now he seems to be noticing her, like she's standing out in some way. That nightmare of his must have really bugged him out. . . .

"Yo, Davis, did you catch that Ms. Landesman had lip-stick, like, all over her teeth today?" Max asks Peter.

"Yeah," Peter responds, feeling like he's on automatic. "That was funny."

Max goes on to describe the sight to Keith and Doug, and Peter continues to watch Meena, who's sucking down her cigarette with so much vigor, it seems like she's on a quest to inhale as much nicotine as possible. Peter suddenly realizes that there is a specific reason—beside the nightmare—that he's noticing Meena now. It's because she looks totally different.

Peter takes another sip of Coke, thinking that the fact that she's alone is one of the major reasons for this. Meena usually hangs with the princessy types and the jocks. She always struck Peter as one of the more well-liked girls in school.

Meena slumps back even more in her seat, resting her head against the window that overlooks the parking lot, and Peter decides that her lack of friends is not the only thing that stands out about her.

When Peter thinks of seeing Meena around school in the past, he remembers her as always laughing. Always smiling. And pretty in a natural sort of way. Peter rests his stocky arms against the coffee-stained table, leaning forward a bit to look at Meena. Even from here, Peter can tell that her small eyes look bloodshot, her dark hair looks stringy, and she definitely is not smiling. Quite the opposite, in fact. And Meena has always been very thin and petite, but her cheeks look totally sunken in. Too thin.

Peter rubs at the back of his neck, feeling a strange, slight pull to go over to her. Maybe it's because of the nightmare. Or maybe it's simply because he can recognize the misery she's obviously feeling. But of course, Peter doesn't move. It would be totally weird. He and Meena used to be friends—when they were ten—but he hasn't spoken to her in years. What would they have to say to each other now?

Just as Peter's about to finally look away from her and

involve himself in whatever it is his friends are talking about, Meena does the craziest thing. She takes her cigarette out of her mouth, contemplates it for a second, and then presses it into the inside of her arm. As Meena's entire face turns bright red and she lifts off the cigarette, Peter almost wheels right over there to help her on impulse. But he sees Norma, the waitress, rush over to Meena before he even moves, pulling the cigarette out of Meena's hand and grabbing some ice out of Meena's glass.

Peter sits there, stunned, as Norma wraps the ice in a napkin and presses it against Meena's burn. Meena's expression barely changes—she almost looks like a robot as Norma holds the ice to her arm—and Peter feels a pit begin to form in his stomach. What the hell is wrong with her?

"Hey, what's going on over there?" Doug asks, craning his neck to try to figure out what Peter's looking at. "Are we missing something?"

Peter takes his gaze off Meena. He looks down and focuses on the three soggy onion rings that are left on the plate in the middle of the table. "No," he says. "I was just spacing out."

The truth is, if Doug knew what Peter just witnessed, he *would* think that he was missing out. Someone putting out a cigarette on their arm is just the kind of thing that Doug would find hilarious.

Peter swallows, realizes he's holding his breath, and then forces himself to let it out. No matter what he used to think, seeing someone miserable is not a form of entertainment.

•••

Jeremy rushes into his empty, quiet house. Well, almost empty. Jeremy's dog, Pablo, is here, and he comes running over to greet Jeremy.

"Hey, boy," Jeremy says, bending down to scratch the big retriever behind his ears. He then drops his backpack on the small table in the foyer, heading into the kitchen and grabbing the bottle of Gatorade out of the big, Sub-Zero fridge. Jeremy's parents are at the halfway house and his sister is at a friend's.

Jeremy glances at the clock on the stove as he continues to drink. 4:37. He wipes at his sweaty forehead and grimaces. Football practice was short today, and Jeremy didn't bother to take a shower at school. He wanted to get home in time to give Tara a call before he went over to meet his parents for dinner and she headed over to her grandparents'. The cheerleaders were getting out early as well, and if Jeremy timed it right, Tara should be finishing up right about now.

As Jeremy pulls the cordless out of its cradle on the wall, he knows that he is just a little bit pathetic, having to make sure he speaks to Tara every evening after having seen her at school all day. But he can't help it. Tara's his best friend, and there's no one he enjoys talking to more.

Jeremy sits down on the upholstered bench by the square breakfast table as he dials Tara's cell number. He grabs a paper towel off the wooden holder on the shelf behind him, wiping his face dry as he listens to Tara's phone ring.

"Hello?" Tara sounds out of breath as she answers.

Jeremy can hear many girls' voices—laughter, shrieks, conversation—muffled in the background.

"Hey. It's me," Jeremy says. He gives the panting Pablo a pat on the head. "You still at practice?"

"Hi, you," Tara says, her voice sounding light and airy. Jeremy can picture her smiling on the other end. "I'm just getting out of the locker room. Hold on a sec."

There's a lot of noise on the line and then moments later she's back.

"Okay. I'm outside now," Tara says. "I thought you were going straight to the halfway house after practice."

Jeremy scratches the back of his neck. "I know. But Coach ended practice early, and I wanted to get you before you went to dinner at your grandparents', so—"

"Jeremy! That's so sweet," Tara gushes.

Jeremy smiles to himself. He loves that he knows exactly what to do to make Tara happy. It's not that hard, actually. "Yeah, well, I'm not going to get to see much of you these next few days. Tomorrow night you're baby-sitting, and Friday you have that girls' night."

Tara laughs. "You don't sound so happy about it," she teases.

Jeremy tugs at the front of his damp T-shirt. "Should I be? What are you girls going to do, anyway? Cruise around and look for cute guys?"

"Yeah, right," Tara responds. "Don't worry about Friday. We'll probably just rent romantic comedies and eat tons of junk food."

"And this is something you want to do?" Jeremy asks jokingly.

"Shut up." Tara laughs. "Besides, I'm the one who should be worried. You're going to that Kennedy party, aren't you?"

Jeremy shrugs. He'd sort of pushed the party to the back of his mind, not giving it much thought. "Haven't decided," he says.

"You should go. It'll be fun," Tara tells him. "Wait a minute. What am I saying? What if some hot blond tries to seduce you?"

Jeremy chuckles. "Then I'll tell her she's wasting her time."

"Wow. You *do* always know exactly what to say."

"On that note, I gotta go," Jeremy says, glancing at the clock.

"Okay, sweetie," Tara says. "Have a good night."

"You too," Jeremy says. "Say hi to the grandparents. Bye."

"Bye."

Jeremy places the phone back on its cradle, then heads out of the kitchen, Pablo running up behind him. He has just enough time for a quick shower before going over to the halfway house. He grabs his backpack off the foyer table as he jogs up the stairs, taking them two at a time.

But when Jeremy gets to his bedroom and drops his bag on his bed, he hesitates for a moment, staring at the backpack. He walks over to it, unzips the front pocket, and fishes around inside the pocket until he finds what he's looking for—a crumpled-up scrap of paper. He unravels the paper to find Josh Strauss's phone number. Josh gave it to Jeremy as they were leaving on Sunday so that he could call him about the party.

As Jeremy stares at Josh's small, neat handwriting, the thought of going to a Kennedy party without Tara by his side makes him feel a little nervous. A little off balance. But then Jeremy tells himself that if he can't manage another school's party without Tara, then he really is pathetic.

What the hell, Jeremy thinks, embarrassed for turning this whole thing into such a big deal. He decides to go for it. Josh isn't working today, so all Jeremy has to do is just call him up and tell him he'll head over to the party with him and Chris. How hard can that be?

Apparently it is just a teensy bit hard since Jeremy decides to put off calling. He has to jump into the shower now. He definitely needs one. But Jeremy will call Josh later.

●●●

"I'm fine," Meena says, holding an ice cube wrapped in a napkin to the cigarette burn on her arm. "Really. Thanks for the ice."

Norma places her hands on her hips—hips that look like they are about to bulge right out of her light pink uniform. "Now, why'd you do that?" she asks, the lines around her hazel-green eyes deepening as she frowns.

Meena picks up the piece of ice and looks down at her arm, staring at the red, inflamed circle that she created. Her muddled, confused responses to Norma's question crowd her brain. *To hurt myself—to feel so much physical pain that I drown the rest of it out. To bruise myself, harm myself, make myself ugly so he won't come near me again. To force a trip to the hospital so that I won't have to go over there tonight.*

But Meena knows this burn didn't accomplish anything. It's small and not *that* unsightly. It stings just a little bit. It comes nowhere near the hurt she feels inside. And there's no way it's going to get her out of baby-sitting tonight. The Claytons are her parents' friends. That's why she started sitting for them in the first place. And as long as she's not hemorrhaging or running a fever of 104, they're going to make her fulfill her obligation.

Meena looks back up at Norma. She shrugs. "I was just messing around. Seeing what it felt like."

Norma shakes her head and rolls her eyes. She pushes a loose strand of her graying hair behind her ear. "Well, you got your answer, didn't you? Keep that ice pressed up against it, okay, honey?"

Meena nods. She places the ice back on her arm. "Okay."

Norma turns and heads off to a table a few booths away, grabbing her little pad of paper and pencil out of her apron as she walks. Meena slumps back in her seat, laying her skinny arm on the table in front of her and resting her head against the window, still holding the ice to her burn.

The truth is, Meena doesn't know why she did what she did, why she felt the overwhelming urge to burn herself, other than it was something to do. Something other than thinking. Something other than dreading tonight.

Meena sits up straight again. Looks out the window, stares at the people getting into their cars. What if there *is* something she can do to herself, though? Something that will make her repulsive to Steven. Something that will make him never want her again.

Or what if there's something she can do to show that she's an incapable baby-sitter? So that she'll never have to go to the Claytons' house alone again? Let Trace stay up late or forget to give him his dinner.

Meena's playing with these thoughts, twisting them around in her brain, when she spots Dana and Luke through the window. They've just stepped out of their cars and are heading right for the Falls Diner's entrance. Meena quickly tosses the piece of ice back into her glass and tucks her burn mark under the table, wishing more than anything that she could hide her shame, her pain, and her anger as easily as she can hide the wound. When Meena's around her friends, she feels exposed, like they know somehow, and she wishes that she could just get out of here without them seeing her. But she's in plain view of the door. Meena glances around the diner, tries to figure another way out. Unless—

"Meen! What are you doing here?"

Meena's throat swells up. There is no unless. She's forced to pretend to be a normal person.

Meena looks up at Dana, who asked the question and is now dropping into the bench across from her. Luke scoots in a second later, next to Dana. "Hanging out," Meena says. She tries very, very hard to sound normal. Like her old self.

"Why aren't you at swim practice?" Luke asks.

Meena's stomach falls. There goes sounding like her old self. She carefully pulls her gaze away from Luke's blue eyes and looks out the window instead. "I quit the team."

"What?" Dana exclaims.

"You're kidding," Luke pipes in. "Why?"

Because I can't do it anymore, Meena thinks. *I can't do anything anymore. Because I'm a worthless, dirty failure and I might as well just drop off the face of the earth.* She lightly fingers her burn under the table, tracing the circular mark. "I'd rather not talk about it," Meena says, looking back to her friends.

Luke and Dana's dumbfounded reactions prove once again that they think she's gone crazy. Certifiable. Meena's cheeks burn as she feels four eyes staring at her, trying to figure her out.

"But Meena, you're the best swimmer on the team," Dana says, her eyebrows scrunched in confused concern. "Do you really want to give that up?"

"Seriously," Luke says. "Swimming used to be the only thing you talked about."

Meena is silent. She lifts up her nonburned arm and takes the napkin off the table, crumpling it into a ball in her hand. She's about to open her mouth to respond, to say *something,* when Luke bursts out, "Jesus, Meen. Smoke much?"

Meena follows Luke's line of vision to see the glass ash-tray to the left of her, filled with ashes and cigarette stubs. *Crap*, she thinks, her stomach sinking. Why didn't she think to hide it? Since Sunday she's been smoking every-where, not just at home. But her friends haven't actually seen her with a cigarette until this moment, and it will just be one more reason for them to pressure her.

"I was bored," Meena manages. "It was something to do."

"Something to do?" Dana leans forward, opening her eyes wide and laying her hands flat on the table. "Meena, you hate smoke. You always make a big show of waving it away when someone's smoking near you."

"I know. . . ."

"Look, there's obviously something wrong," Dana says, looking Meena directly in the eye. "First you stop hanging out with us, then you start drinking, and now you're smoking? I hate to harp on this, Meen, but tell us what's wrong. We're your friends."

Meena's insides feel tenuous. Fragile. Like she might col-lapse at any moment. Meena's grip tightens around the crumpled-up napkin and she bites the inside of her mouth, doing everything she can to hold it in. To prevent herself from crying. She shakes her head, not able to get any words out.

"Is it something at home?" Dana asks tentatively. "Are your parents fighting or something?"

"Dana, really," Meena croaks out. She clears her throat and tries to look at her friend but can't lift her heavy eye-lids. "I don't want to talk about it. I'm fine, okay?"

"You're obviously not," Dana says. Her voice is full of concern and she's almost begging. "We want to be here for you, but you have to start letting us in. Talk to us."

Meena wishes it was that simple. She wishes she could just talk to her friends, get them to help her. But she already knows—just by the way they're looking at her now, by the way they've been looking at her for days—that they think she's nuts. And they'll definitely think that it's her fault.

"You gotta admit you've been acting like a totally different person," Luke puts in, pushing some of his shaggy blond hair away from his eyes.

Meena stiffens. She is a different person. And they know. Dana doesn't want to protect her or comfort her; she just wants to hear her say it out loud. Wants to hear Meena admit that she's a slut. But she's not going to do it. She's not going to say the words and see their faces change. See them look at her with disgust and horror.

Meena slides out of the booth. She's done. She doesn't have the energy to try to pretend anymore. To try to act like she's the Meena they used to know. And if they're not even buying it, what's the point?

Meena grabs her backpack, shouldering it. "Just forget about it, guys," Meena tells her stunned-looking friends. "Give up. I'm not worth your time."

Meena can see that both Dana and Luke are about to say something, but she turns and walks off before they have the chance.

CHAPTER EiGHT

Meena sits on the edge of her bed, hands folded in her lap, picking at her cuticles, staring at her poster of the American women's World Cup soccer team on the opposite wall.

She is killing time so that she'll show up late to the Claytons' tonight. Maybe that way, Steven will be gone by the time she gets there. Maybe she won't see him at all. Meena lets out a shaky breath as nausea overcomes her. Maybe, maybe, maybe . . .

Meena looks down to the ground. Maybe isn't good enough for Meena anymore. Maybe leaves too many possibilities open. Her throat dries out and she feels like she can't swallow. Too many terrifying possibilities.

"Meena?"

Meena stands at the sound of her father's voice, her muscles tightening. She goes to her door, unlocks it— Meena never used to lock her door, but it's become a habit recently—and peeks her head out into the hall, where her father is standing at the head of the stairs. "Yes?"

"What's the story?" her father demands, leaning one hand on the carved wooden banister. "It's seven. Shouldn't you be at the Claytons' right now?"

Meena sits down on her bed again and looks up at her father shakily. "Dad, I'm not feeling so well," she says.

The irritation at her lateness falls from his face, replaced by concern. *This might work,* Meena thinks, her heart daring to hope. *Please, Dad, just let me stay home.*

"What is it?" her father asks. He strides into the room and over to her, putting his palm to her forehead. "You don't feel warm."

How could she not feel warm? She's sweating with anxiety.

"It's just my stomach," Meena says, her voice sounding weak. "It hasn't felt right all day."

Her father takes a step back and studies her face. Meena has to look away, even as she tries not to. She's never been a person who could look her parents in the eye and lie.

"Are you just trying to get out of sitting tonight?" he asks, arms crossed over his chest. "Because if you are, it's a little late, isn't it? You could have at least had the decency to call Steven and Lydia earlier and give them time to find someone else."

Decency. Decency. Decency. The word keeps repeating itself in Meena's mind until it sounds weird. Until it means nothing.

"Dad, I—"

"Get your stuff together, Meena," he says, looking down at her with his patented stern expression. "Come on. Let's go."

"Fine," Meena says, wanting to burst into tears as she stands. She feels like her father is sending her off to the slaughter.

She grabs her tote bag off her bed and walks over to look for her car keys in her desk drawer, her knees feeling weak. Her father watches her from the door frame.

"Meen, Steven and Lydia were nice enough to give you this gig so you could make some cash. You have to be responsible about this."

Meena's heart drops. She can't stand feeling like she's letting her parents down. And she knows that if they ever found out what she really was, their feelings would go far beyond mere disappointment. She's glad that her back is to her father as she scoops up her keys so that he can't see the tears in her eyes. The guilt of everything she's done seems to squeeze her lungs so hard, she can barely breathe. Her parents have been friends with the Claytons for so long. Her father would never be able to understand how something like this could happen. Not with his dear old friend Steven. He would know it was Meena's fault.

He'd probably blame it on my genes, Meena thinks. She blinks to try to make her tears invisible, then turns and looks at her father, a tall, hefty, Caucasian man who looks nothing like her. *He'd blame it on the fact that I'm adopted and that he doesn't understand how my brain works.*

Meena hefts her bag over her shoulder and walks past her father to head into the hall and down the stairs, mumbling out a "sorry" as she passes him. Meena knows that her fears about her parents disowning her are well-founded. Steven has even told her he's read cases about that very thing happening—parents who adopted children from other countries who ended up giving those children up because they'd turned out to be too much to handle. Too much of a burden.

Meena jogs down the stairs, despair and misery clouding around her. Even if her parents didn't disown her, they *could* stop loving her. After all, she's not of their blood. She's not really theirs.

"Say hi to Steven and Lyd for me," Meena's dad calls from upstairs, poking his head over the banister. "And call if you need anything."

"Okay," Meena responds as she opens the front door.

She steps outside, but before she closes the door, Meena hears her father add, "And don't forget to apologize for being late!"

Meena takes another step, lets the front door slam behind her. She looks at her watch. 7:03. She'll only be ten or twelve minutes late. Maybe that will be enough, though. Maybe he'll be gone.

Meena walks down her porch steps and heads over to her car. As she gets in and starts it up, she blasts the radio, turns it up high to drown out all of her horrible feelings, to calm her nerves, and as she drives to the Claytons she prays and prays and prays that Steven won't be there.

But none of it works.

Because when Meena pulls up at the Claytons' minutes later, she sees that both cars are parked in the driveway.

He's home.

Still, Meena does feel one small dose of relief as she steps out of her car and sees Lydia hurrying out the front door, little Trace in her arms, Steven walking up behind her. Meena grabs her bag out of the back, locks the Honda. At least they're on their way out. And they're both kind of dressed up. They're probably going out together. Which means they'll be coming home together. Hopefully.

"Meena, there you are," Lydia says, meeting Meena on the front path.

"Mee-na!" Trace exclaims, his blue eyes opening wide.

"Sorry I'm late," Meena says, taking Trace in her arms. She kisses the top of the boy's head and does everything she can to avoid looking at Steven, who she can feel gazing at her over Lydia's shoulder. Her skin crawls when she realizes this is probably going to become a normal thing— Meena trying to act like everything's fine to Lydia, while Steven watches her longingly.

"That's okay, sweetie. You're usually on time." Lydia bends down to give her son a quick kiss on the cheek, her silver bangles jangling as she moves her arms. "But you'll have to excuse us as we run off. We're late for an anniversary party."

A little bit of tension flows out of Meena. Her narrow shoulders relax. They definitely *are* going out together. That means no alone time with Steven. "Go ahead," Meena says.

"Bye, guys," Lydia says, already walking toward the cars. "Be good, Trace. We should be home by ten."

"Bye-bye!" Trace calls out, wriggling a bit in Meena's arms.

"Okay," Meena says, waving good-bye to Lydia. But Meena can't ignore the fact that Steven is not following his wife. He's hesitating. Standing there. Just looking at Meena.

Steven takes a step closer and Meena notices that he's shaved. No scruff. But he looks vile to her. He touches her arm—it's not bare, she's wearing a windbreaker—but his touch still sends waves of repulsion traveling up and down her spine.

"Hey, Meen," he says. "Night, Trace." He bends down, kisses Trace's pale forehead, then smiles right into Meena's eyes. As if he's laughing at her. "I'll see you later," he says.

Steven jogs off to go join his wife, who's already waiting in the car. Meena tightens her hold on Trace and hurries into the house, wanting to get out of Steven's view as quickly as possible.

"That my daddy," Trace says as Meena lets him down in the front hall.

Meena just nods, but she doesn't say a word.

• • •

"I'll see you later."

A couple of hours have passed and Trace is now asleep in his room, but those four words still reverberate in Meena's brain. When Steven says something like that, he means it. He *will* see Meena later. Alone.

Meena closes her eyes and grasps the armrests of the

antique rocking chair she's sitting in, trying to slow her racing heart. But that's almost impossible when all she can think about is how she's going to get away from Steven— or not be able to get away from Steven.

No. Meena opens her eyes. Stares at the battered old couch across from her. She has to get away from Steven. She has to think of something. She can't let what happened the other night happen again.

The thought of it, of Steven touching her, forcing himself inside her, causes Meena to start to sweat, to feel like she might faint, and Meena tells herself she has to calm down. Get those thoughts out of her mind. Because they only make her weak, and she has to be strong. Or try to be, at least.

She leans down and pulls her hefty history textbook out of her tote bag, thinking that maybe doing some homework will distract her for a moment. Clear her brain of the nightmares. So she turns to page seventy-three and begins to read.

A moment later—after Meena's read the same sentence four times and still hasn't absorbed it—she hears the sound of a car approaching the house and her heart jumps. The car soon passes right by, not stopping at all, but Meena's nervous system has now shifted into overdrive and her pulse is racing like crazy. She takes a deep breath, manages to calm herself just a little bit, and rereads that same sentence.

Just as she's getting to the last word, the floor lamp between the couch and the armchair flickers and Meena slams the book shut, realizing this is useless. She is way too freaked out to concentrate on her homework. She's about to stand up and turn the lamp off, but it stops flickering, so she puts her book away and grabs her knitting instead. Knitting is the one thing that even comes close to calming her these days.

Meena starts to work the needles, continuing on with the blue-and-green scarf she started weeks ago. Her heart still beats at double speed, and her hands are a little shaky, but at least she's able to complete the stitches.

The lamp flickers again, but this time Meena ignores it, intent on losing herself and losing her fear in her knitting. She's not going to let that stupid lamp shake her again, pull her out of her one minute of relative peace. So she keeps working, satisfied with how neat and orderly the stitches are. Even the sound of the needles hitting each other is calming. Just a soft, repetitive clicking.

Then Meena smells something, something weird. She stops moving the needles and sniffs the air. It's the scent of something burning.

Meena looks up from her knitting and glances around. And then she sees it.

It's the standing lamp. It flickers once again, then Meena sees a spark, hears a sizzle. Meena knows this is not good. Bluish flecks of light spray out of the frayed lamp cord. Then a hiss. Spark. Sizzle. No, not good at all.

That sensation of dread prickles the skin on her bony arms. But Meena doesn't move. She can't. She just watches.

It all happens so fast. Even though she saw it coming a

millisecond earlier, Meena is now stunned—her breath catches as the sparks buzzing off the faulty cord suddenly spread into a flame. The upholstered skirt of the chair on the other side of the lamp—Steven's favorite chair—curls, seemingly trying to shrink away from the heat. But the fabric can't move quickly enough. It catches fire.

Meena is transfixed. Even though she felt nothing but pure fear the first couple of hours she was in this house, she now feels strangely calm as she sits in the rocking chair on the opposite side of the living room, cool knitting needles still in her hands, the half-made scarf tumbling out of her lap.

"I'll see you later. . . ."

Right before Meena's eyes the flames dance and spread across the fabric. Steven's chair—the one where he made Meena sit in his lap that first time, when she thought it was fun and harmless—ignites. Meena is still—too still—as the chair crackles. And sears. And soars into flame.

Meena's dark oval eyes widen and stay that way. She hears her heart thudding now; it is in fact all she hears as she watches the flames swell to the tattered brown couch. The knitting needles slip from Meena's hands. In the depths of her mind, she knows she should be scared, but she's not. *I should be running,* she thinks vaguely. *I should get out of here.*

But she's mesmerized. She can feel the heat of the fire against her sunken cheeks. Her long-sleeved cotton shirt feels heavy and sticky. But still Meena does not move. Somehow she *can't* move.

Meena remembers the freckle-faced fireman who came

to her fourth-grade class. She recalls how he instructed them to prepare In Case of Fire. Make sure your parents have smoke alarms and fire extinguishers in the house. If a fire breaks out, leave immediately and do not go back in. Call 911 from the neighbors' house.

Meena has been instructed what to do in this situation.

But then, that female cop—Officer O'Neill—had also told Meena's ninth-grade PE class what to do In Case of Attack. In Case of Abuse. Tell someone. Anyone.

Abused. Attacked. Steven says that Meena led him on. *She* flirted with *him*. What was he supposed to do? How could he resist? Really. It's all her fault. And if it's her fault, it's not abuse. It's not an attack. So there's no reason to tell anyone.

When she was younger, she thought that Steven was handsome. And funny. Sort of like Harrison Ford in those Indiana Jones movies that her mother liked so much. She knows she was attracted to him. Even Holly remembers.

I have to get away from Steven tonight. I can't let it happen again. . . .

Guilt. Anger. Fear. Loss. A cocktail of emotions spills through Meena's dulled veins as the fire gets bigger. As the room grows hotter.

But when the bookshelf behind the couch catches on fire and Steven's prized stacks of leather photo albums shrivel, Meena feels a quick shot of something else. Relief? Satisfaction?

Her fingers clasp the wooden edge of her chair, her eyes beginning to sting and water from the smoke. Steven's life—his work, his travels with Lydia—is packed into those thick albums. Out of one of those tomes, Steven once showed Meena photos of Vietnam—the place where she was born and of which her parents know very little. He'd told her what women were like in her country. Beautiful, sexual, coy. He'd touched her face and she'd felt a thrill of excitement. Followed quickly by a thump of foreboding. Her first. The first of many.

Now, as the albums melt together, destroying Steven's memories, Meena feels a smile tug at her lips. He deserves this. Deserves this for what he did to her.

And suddenly something wakes up inside her. She does not want to burn. She does not want to die.

Then she remembers Trace.

Finally the adrenaline kicks in and tells Meena to get the hell out of there. She jumps off her seat, trips over her half-knitted scarf, and scrambles back up, running right up the back stairway to Trace's small room.

Trace is asleep. He is oblivious to the danger surrounding him, even as Meena can feel the oppressive heat broiling his pale yellow bedroom. She scoops Trace up and hurries out of his room, down the stairs, and out the back door.

Miraculously, even with all the movement, even with the plunge into the cool air, Trace does not stir; his body is slack against Meena's as she sprints across the Claytons' barren backyard toward the back of the neighbors' brick house.

Panting, shaking, Meena is yards away from the

Davises' back door when something in her makes her stop for a moment. And look.

Meena turns around, still holding Trace's warm body close to her chest, his halo of soft blond hair in her hand. All of the blood drains from her face—she almost faints— as she sees the enormous blaze that the Claytons' house has become.

Meena hugs Trace tighter, clinging to him. She almost feels like he's carrying her and not the other way around as she sees the hungry flames devour his home.

The fear is gone. The satisfaction is gone. Even the guilt, at that moment, is gone. All there is now is the unfamiliar sensation of relief.

• • •

Peter can't believe his eyes.

He was sitting at the end of the bed, playing some mindless Sega game, when he casually turned his head to look out the window, and he saw it. The fire. The huge, towering flames filling up the frame of his window. The smoke billowing out of the neighbors' blazing roof. He can smell it now. The smell of a family's home burning.

Peter is speechless. He's never seen anything like this. The enormity of it. The total destruction. And then he sees something else, some*one* else, that makes this scene even more surreal.

It's Meena. And she's running away from the fire and toward Peter's house, toward his back door. There's a little boy in her arms—Trace Clayton, probably—and even from here Peter can see that Meena looks petrified. Her small, dark eyes appear startled, opened wide.

As Meena runs closer, an image of her burning her arm in the diner that day pops into Peter's brain. That image then dissolves into the ten-year-old image of her, the one from Peter's nightmare. The one where she's asking him to help her.

A chill electrifies Peter's body and he realizes he has to do something. He uses his arms to push himself up more so that he can slide into his wheelchair, which sits next to his bed. But after a second of maneuvering, Peter knows it's going to take him too long, it always does, and he yells out to his parents, who are out in the living room.

"Mom! Dad! There's a fire next door!"

Peter can hear the TV through his thin wall and he realizes they probably can't even hear him. His dad has most likely fallen asleep with a beer in his hands and his mom is probably too absorbed in some sappy Lifetime movie of the week.

Peter curses under his breath. He feels the sweat on his forehead as he continues to position himself so that he can get into his chair. The stench of the smoke, of the fire, becomes more pungent and Peter wonders how his parents don't smell it. Why they don't wake the hell up?

"Mom! Dad! Fire!" he yells, this time much louder.

He looks out the window, sees that Meena is now inches away from his back door, looking totally flipped out. Trace is crying and Meena appears weak. Like she might collapse or faint.

"Dammit," Peter mutters, cursing the fact that he can't just jump out of bed like a normal person. But finally he manages; he slides himself into his chair. At the same moment that he hears knocking at the back door, he hears the sound of his mom's footsteps running through the kitchen to his room.

Peter has started to wheel himself toward his doorway when his mom swings open his door. She takes one look out his window and holds her hand up to her mouth. "Oh my God," she gasps, all color draining from her face.

Peter's father runs up right behind her, and his dark brown eyes open wide at the sight of the blaze. They all hear the sound of Meena knocking, and Peter's father pulls open the back door and quickly ushers Meena inside, placing a big, protective arm around her small shoulders. Peter's mom takes the crying Trace out of Meena's hands and tries to calm him, soothingly massaging his back.

They all rush into the living room, Peter wheeling himself in. The next few moments are a chaotic blur—Peter's mom sits Meena down on the couch while Peter's father calls the fire department and his coworkers at the police department. Trace's crying has died down to a whimper and Meena quietly answers Peter's mom's questions: *Yes, she was baby-sitting. The Claytons are at an anniversary party. No, she doesn't know where. They left the phone number for her, but it's inside the house. . . . Yes, her parents should be home. . . .*

Peter wheels himself next to Meena as she speaks. He can see her hands shaking, can hear the tremble in her voice; he can practically smell the fear shooting out of her eyes. He can recognize that trauma-produced fear because he has experienced it himself. He has lived it.

Peter's mom hurries into the kitchen to make some calls, presumably to Meena's parents. She takes Trace with her as she darts away, still holding the little boy in her arms. Peter looks to Meena. She's focused on her hands, fidgeting with her thumb ring, and he doesn't know what to say to her.

As they sit there silently for a moment and Peter hears the buzz of activity—his parents rushing around, speaking to each other in hushed, panicked voices, making calls and answering them, the sound of the sirens getting louder and louder—Peter is reminded of that time when he and Meena were ten, when they were in *this* very house and—

Peter pulls himself out of the distant memory. That was years ago. Peter is almost seventeen now, Meena is seventeen, and they haven't so much as said hello to each other in years.

Still, she's sitting next to him right now, after having just bolted out of a burning house, looking scared out of her mind. Peter pulls at a loose thread on his chair's armrest, realizing he has to say *something* to her. He has to try to bring her out of the hell she's probably trapped in at the moment.

The sirens get much, much louder, then they cut off all together. Peter rubs the back of his head. "Sounds like the firemen got there already."

Meena glances up from her hands and looks at Peter

148

Really looks at him, like she's searching his face for answers. For explanations. "Yeah," she says.

Peter swallows. The intensity of her fear, of her sadness, cuts right through him, makes him feel like it's hard to breathe. Like it's hard to talk. But now she's watching him, waiting for him to speak, looking like she needs for him to say something. . . .

So he says the only two words that come to mind. "You okay?"

• • •

Meena blinks. Is she okay? Of course, people have been asking her this for days, but from something about the way Peter poses the question, something about the way his serious green eyes seem to be so intent on gathering the truth, Meena doesn't think she can fake it. An image of the bookshelf catching fire flashes before her and she shudders.

"No," Meena responds. She notices that her hair smells like smoke, it smells burnt, and she pushes the dark strands away from her face. "I don't know."

Peter seems unsure of what to say, of what to do, and he rubs his hands up and down against his legs. Meena watches him, wonders if he can feel that, if his legs register any feeling, then quickly looks away, surprised at herself for thinking such a thing at a moment like this.

"Well . . . at least you made it out all right," Peter says. "You know, you and Trace."

Meena nods silently, staring down at her lap. The gravity of what just happened is hitting her now; it's crashing down on her. The Claytons' house, all of their possessions, are most likely burned to a crisp, and Meena could have prevented it if she had just moved sooner. A tight ball begins to grow in Meena's throat as she wonders whether she is a monster, or if Steven's the monster, or if they both are. Meena clasps her hands together, wringing them. Suddenly she doesn't know who the monster is. Or, rather, she knows they both are.

But she is glad she got Trace out of there. Thank God she got Trace out of there.

Meena hears the back door swing open, followed by the sounds of boots clomping on the linoleum floor. She glances up in the direction of the kitchen. "Wow, Pete, it's a mess over there," she can hear a deep male voice say to Peter's father. She can't see anyone from where she and Peter are sitting in the living room, but she figures it's most likely a cop. One of Mr. Davis's fellow officers.

Peter clears his throat, looks over at Meena nervously, running his hand over his light brown, bald head. "You, uh, feel kind of achy?" he asks. "Does your whole body hurt?"

Meena doesn't have to stop and think about this to answer, "Yes." Every muscle in her body feels tired and cranky and worn out, as if she just completed a triathlon. This seems absurd to her, though. All she did was run from the Claytons' house to here. Her entire body shouldn't be crying out in pain. But it is.

"It's the adrenaline draining out of you," Peter explains. "That's normal."

Meena doesn't respond. She's far from understanding what's normal anymore. But still, she is glad to have Peter sitting next to her now, especially as that man who came in talks to Peter's parents in a restrained, concerned voice in the kitchen.

This surprises Meena, that Peter's presence comforts her somewhat, because Meena doesn't like to be around anybody anymore. And also because she and Peter aren't friends—they haven't been for years. But then again, Meena thinks, maybe that's it. She squints at Peter, realizing that it's not hard to remember what he looked like when they were kids, when they were good friends. Aside from his shaved head, Peter's face hasn't changed all that much. Same big eyes. Same long, lean face. Maybe it's good enough, maybe it's better, even, to have someone here who doesn't really know her. "This is Meena, right here," Meena hears Mrs. Davis say as she walks into the room from the kitchen. She's still holding Trace—he's sleeping again—and she carefully places him on the couch next to Meena, sitting down on the other side of him and letting his little blond head rest in her lap. "Meena, this is Chief Flaherty," she says, gesturing to the tall, imposing man who now stands in front of her.

Chief Flaherty takes off his fire helmet and regards Meena with gentle brown eyes. "We've managed to put it out," he informs Meena. "But that was some fire. It devoured the house."

Meena swallows as that ball in her throat grows bigger,

threatening to choke her. So the house *is* destroyed. It *is* burned to a crisp.

What has she done?

Chief Flaherty squats down so that he is eye level with Meena. "You did a great job getting yourself and this little boy out of there, though. That was a very brave thing you did."

As Meena stares back at the fireman, she grasps the armrest with one hand, immediately brought back to that time when she was ten, when *it* happened. Maybe it's because the fireman is talking to her like she's a child or the fact that he's commending her on her bravery, just the way those cops did on that night seven years ago. Or maybe it's because Peter's here, and Peter's parents are, too, and she's sitting on the same green-and-white sofa that she was sitting on that night. Meena shifts, uncomfortable.

"I know this is hard," the fireman says. "But do you know how it started? Did you see anything?"

Meena's mouth opens, but nothing comes out. What is she supposed to say? That she saw it start? That she watched it spread? That she did nothing but stand there? That she even smiled? A chill overtakes her body and she wraps her arms around her knees, pulling them up toward her chest.

The fireman's eyes are filled with kindness. He begins to stand. "If you don't want to talk about it yet—"

Then the doorbell rings and Meena's eyes dart to the door. Mr. Davis opens it and Meena's parents and the Claytons come rushing in—Meena's mom and dad head right toward her and Steven and Lydia run to Trace, waking him up.

"You're okay, you're okay. Thank God you're okay," Meena's father says into her hair. Her parents hug her tightly from either side as she stands up; they kiss her from either side. She can feel the wetness from her mother's tears against her forehead.

Then it builds up inside Meena. That ball in her throat finally disintegrates and she begins to cry. Meena's mother pulls her into a real hug as her father walks off to talk to the Davises. Meena clings to the back of her mother's soft waffle shirt, comforts herself with the smell of her mother's peppermint lotion.

"Meena. Thank you. Thank you for saving Trace."

Meena's mother lets go of her so that Meena can acknowledge the statement. Meena turns and looks at Lydia, who sits on the couch, holding Trace in her lap, clinging to him.

Meena just nods, then shrugs, wiping away some of her tears. There's nothing she can say. She knows she is not a hero. Far from it.

Steven stands up, places a hand on Meena's shoulder. As always, his touch sends shudders down her back, but now there's something else disarming her. It's the way his light blue eyes are regarding her, piercing her. Trying to read her. Meena imagines that Steven knows—that he thinks she caused the fire.

"Yes, thank you," Steven says, his eyes still carefully trained on Meena's.

Meena's stomach lurches. What if he does know? What if he does suspect her? But then, as Steven stands there, his firm, disgusting grip still squared on her shoulder, a part of Meena feels a tiny bit glad. Satisfied. Happy that his precious things are gone forever.

Because that's just how she feels. Gone forever.

But there's also the other part of Meena. The part of her that's terrified. That wonders what Steven thinks, what he knows, what he'll say or do.

Steven leans down and kisses Meena's forehead. He smiles at her gratefully, reaching for the bottom of her chin like she's a child. "Your father would never forgive me if anything ever happened to his beautiful girl," he says.

His eyes bore into hers and Meena feels like she's being turned inside out. As if he can see everything inside her. As if he knows all. Meena is about to look away, but she makes herself stay where she is. She's not going to let him take away the tiny flicker of satisfaction that's still burning somewhere beneath the fear and the guilt. She can't let go of that. Not now.

And so she stares right back at him. She stares back at him until *he* blinks and looks away.

CHAPTER NiNE

The next morning Meena feels a lot calmer. Strangely calm, considering all that has happened. As she sits at the small, round table in the kitchen, eating her cereal, she realizes that this is the first time she's eaten a real breakfast in days. Lately her stomach has felt too screwed up to digest any food first thing in the morning, but today she is actually hungry. Famished.

Maybe that's because it's ten, not seven forty-five like it usually is when she's rushing out of the house. Meena's parents let her sleep in and told her she should stay home from school and rest since she's been through so much. Her parents didn't go to work today, either, saying that they wanted to stay with Meena and make sure she's okay.

Of course, she's not okay. She never will be. But something about what happened last night has quieted her nerves and has allowed her to get a little sleep.

Meena swallows another spoonful of cereal, biting down on the now soggy flakes. It doesn't take her long to figure out what that "something" is. It's the realization that she probably won't have to be alone with Steven for a very long time. At this very moment he's holed up at the Ramada Inn with his family, and from what Meena's parents have been saying this morning, they are not going to be able to move back into their house for a while. Meena doesn't imagine they'll have much need for a baby-sitter.

She's still haunted by the flames of last night, still bears the shame of what she and Steven have done, the shame of what she's done to the Claytons, but the possibility of a Steven-free existence is enough to make her feel a little bit better.

"Do you want anything else, honey?" her mother asks as she walks into the kitchen. She places a hand on the back of Meena's head, smoothing out her long hair. "Want some orange juice? We have some from the farmers' market. Fresh squeezed."

Meena shakes her head. "No. Thanks."

Her mother pulls out the red chair next to Meena's and sits down. She takes one of Meena's hands in her much bigger, much paler ones, clasping it. "How are you feeling? Do you want to talk about it?"

Meena can hear the word her mother doesn't say. The one lingering in the air at the end of her sentence. It's all over her face, as always. *Baby. Do you want to talk about it, baby?*

So even though she saved Trace. Even though, as far as her parents know, she did the responsible, mature, adult thing and got herself and Trace out of there unscathed, she's still going to be coddled. Instead of earning their respect, it's like the fire has set her back.

Meena pulls her hand away so that she can pick up her mug and take a sip of coffee. Her mother is so good in a crisis. She knows how to behave in all situations. She's the first to bring a homemade pie over to the neighbors', the first to send off a condolence card to a friend who's lost a parent. She thrives in this role of post-trauma parent, and Meena knows her mother wants to help her through this one.

If she only knew that last night was the least of Meena's traumas . . . would she still see Meena as a baby then?

"No," Meena responds. "I'm okay."

Meena's mom holds a hand up to Meena's cheek, her wavy dark hair falling over her face as she leans forward. "All right, sweetie. But I'm here if you need me."

Her mother stands, takes the coffeepot over to the sink, and rinses it out. Meena watches her, wondering how true that statement is. Would she really be there, no matter what? Even if Meena told her what really happened?

"Just got off the phone with Steven," Meena's father says as he comes walking through the kitchen door. He shakes his head, runs a hand through his disheveled brown hair. "Man. What a mess."

Meena places her mug down on the table. A nervous feeling plants itself in the pit of her stomach.

Meena's mom glances at her dad over her shoulder as she dries off the coffeepot with a dishrag. "What's going on?"

"Pretty much everything's destroyed," Meena's father says. "And the investigators are over there now, looking into the cause of the fire. Lyd's all upset because they have to investigate the possibility of arson."

"What?" Meena's mother blurts out as Meena's heart hits the floor. "They don't think that Meena—"

"It's just routine procedure, sweetie," Meena's father says, always rational. He looks at Meena. "And no one thinks you had anything to do with it, okay?"

Meena feels herself nod.

"It's just the first possibility they investigate, that's all." He takes off his glasses and pinches the bridge of his nose before putting them back on. "Still, it is a little absurd. Why would anyone purposely start that fire? It's just a family home. You'd have to be a crazy person."

Meena suddenly feels very queasy. She looks down at her bowl of cereal, and the sight of the floating flakes makes her feel even more nauseous. What if the investigators find that the fire could have been prevented? That *Meena* could have prevented it from getting out of control? That it's her fault the house was leveled? Fear and dread and guilt begin to creep their way into her bones.

You'd have to be a crazy person. . . .

Meena's mother lets out a sigh. "Like you said, it's just routine procedure."

Meena stands. She can't listen to her parents talk about this. She can't wonder what the firemen will find out. Because the anticipation alone will kill her.

"I'm going upstairs," she says, quickly putting her bowl in the sink. "I'm going back to sleep."

Her father places a hand on her shoulder before she can dart off. "You okay?"

"Yes," Meena says, moving away. "Just tired." And then she quickly walks off so that she doesn't have to hear any more discussion of the investigation.

But she's just at the bottom of the stairs and not completely out of earshot when she hears her mom say to her dad, "Maybe we shouldn't talk about this in front of her."

A chill races down Meena's spine and she runs up the stairs. All of this feels too eerily familiar. And she knows why. It's all the echoes of that time when she was ten, when the police officers were trying to figure out exactly what happened after the accident. Her parents were incensed that the cops were questioning children, and Meena overheard them talking about it. For weeks Meena worried. She was terrified that she might get found out.

Just like she is now.

Meena rushes into her room, closes the door behind her, and crawls into her bed, burying herself under her purple comforter. She curls up into the fetal position and wishes she could just disappear.

The brief moment of calm is long over.

• • •

Jeremy sits at his desk in classroom 235, his legs bouncing nervously under his desk. Mr. Rearick, Jeremy's creative-writing teacher, is about to hand back the stories that the class submitted last week, and Jeremy can hardly contain himself.

Mr. Rearick, in his usual slow, very carefully paced way, is perched on the desk at the front of the room, explaining the criteria he used to grade the students' work and going over his revision policy.

But Jeremy is too anxious to absorb any of it. Besides, if this story is as good as Jeremy thinks it is, he won't even need to revise it. He spent a lot of time on the piece, much more time than he usually spends on any sort of homework, and he is particularly proud of it.

Rearick had hammered home the write-what-you-know point so many times that Jeremy finally started to fear that he didn't know anything worth writing about. Then, when he'd been sure his head was going to explode from brainstorming, he'd realized there was one thing he knew everything about—sports. Sports and the pressure to succeed. So he wrote a story about a guy named Paul who was the star of his basketball team at school, who had everyone cheering for him and believing in him, but who hated basketball. He was good at it, but it just wasn't him. In the end, Paul had to decide whether to be true to himself and quit the team or whether to play in the championship game and keep his teammates, school, and community happy.

Paul had played in the game. And scored the winning shot, of course.

Finally Mr. Rearick stands, and Jeremy perks up, thinking

the teacher is at last going to hand out the stack of papers he holds in his hands. But then Mr. Rearick hesitates and proceeds to launch into a minilecture about the value of constructive criticism.

Jeremy rolls his eyes, slumping all the way back into his seat. He feels like running up there and just grabbing the story out of the teacher's pale hands. Jeremy taps his pen against his spiral notebook, realizing that this feeling of actually wanting to get homework back is completely new for him. And it's pretty ironic that it's happening in creative writing, of all classes.

Jeremy wasn't even going to sign up for this elective at the end of last year. He always had a curiosity about writing; he even thought he might be good at it. But part of him worried that it would be too much of a sensitive-guy class and that his friends and teammates would tease him for enrolling in it. But one night Jeremy read this really cool book of short stories and he knew he had to give it a try. So he signed up. As he suspected might happen, Jeremy did take some good-natured ribbing from people like Mike Chumsky for wanting to be a "poet boy," but that soon passed. And Jeremy has been loving everything about this class since day one.

Well, almost everything. Except for Rearick's particularly annoying habit of taking forever to hand things out . . .

Finally. Jeremy sits up straight. Chews on the end of his pen. And waits.

"Good work, Charlene," Mr. Rearick says, handing

one paper to the girl in front of Jeremy. "Interesting story," Mr. Rearick comments, dropping another paper on Jared Lamott's desk.

Mr. Rearick's commentary continues and Jeremy is almost the very last to get his story back—his is on the bottom of the pile. When the teacher does make it over to Jeremy's desk, he gives him a thin smile. "Good start, Jeremy," Mr. Rearick says.

Jeremy's stomach falls as the paper lands in the middle of his desk. He just stares at it for a moment, dumbfounded, as Mr. Rearick walks away. *Good start?* What the *hell* does that mean? Jeremy tugs on the collar of his green crewneck sweater. This wasn't a start. This was the finished product. A completed story.

Taking in a deep breath, Jeremy quickly flips the pages, passing through all of the red-inked comments marked throughout the story, and just skips to the end to find out his grade. And when he does see it, when he does take in that big, red letter, Jeremy is shocked.

B-minus. Jeremy blinks. He can't believe it. A B-minus. All of that hard work, all of that effort. He'd even canceled plans with Tara one night to work on the story. He'd thought, no, he'd been sure he was going to bring home his first A of the semester. . . .

Jeremy chews on the inside of his lip as he reads Rearick's comments: *A good jumping-off point, Jeremy. You have the beginnings of a real story here. But you need to take more risks, stop holding back. The main character, Paul, is lacking depth. He feels restrained and a bit forced. Come see me if you'd like to do a revision.*

Lacking depth? Restrained? Forced? Jeremy clenches his jaw. He glances up at Mr. Rearick, who is in the process of writing an assignment on the blackboard. Jeremy feels like tossing the paper at Rearick's balding head. Does his teacher realize that the story is semiautobiographical? That Paul is really Jeremy? He can't be *that* restrained if he's based on himself. That forced. And Rearick thought all this story merited was a B-minus?

How can Jeremy be so crappy at something he likes so much, something he puts so much effort into?

Screw it, Jeremy thinks. He picks up the paper and stuffs it into his backpack, having zero intention of revising the thing.

• • •

Thursday, as Peter sits in the cafeteria during lunch, a half-eaten hamburger on the long narrow table in front of him, all he can think about is last night. The fire. Meena. All the sirens, all the chaos.

Peter is eating with Max, Keith, and Doug, who are in the middle of discussing the merits of the new Godsmack album, but Peter has completely zoned out of the conversation, opting instead to remember the details of last night. Details that a lot of people would probably choose to forget.

But not Peter. He picks at the hamburger bun, tearing off a small piece of the soft bread and popping it in his mouth. He can vividly picture the frightened, desperate look in Meena's dark eyes. He can remember the smell of the smoke, of the flames. The sound of Trace crying.

Last night was intense, no question about that. But here's the weird thing: as horrible and as gut-wrenching as it was, being thrown into that tragedy, waiting there with Meena, made Peter feel more alive than he has in weeks.

Peter knows it's lame, but he can't help but think about that nightmare—the one where Meena, along with his other childhood friends, was asking Peter to help her. And last night he did. Sort of. His parents helped her, at least. Not that there's anything to say about that, anything to make of it. It's not like Peter believes in fate. Or God. But still. The whole thing is weird. Eerie. A chill runs down Peter's neck even as he thinks about it.

A crumpled-up napkin pelts Peter on the nose and he snaps out of it. He looks right at Doug, who sits across from him and who obviously threw the makeshift ball.

"Hey, space boy," Doug says, his brown eyes mocking. "You going to come down from whatever the hell planet you're floating on?"

Peter's broad shoulders tense up. Lately, the way his friends talk, the way they joke, completely annoys him. Gets under his skin in a major way. Peter doesn't know why. He just knows that he finds them grating. But Peter tries to shrug it off. These past couple of days his friends have made him feel like he's becoming uptight, and that's one thing Peter definitely does not want to be.

"Sorry. I was just thinking about last night. You know, the fire."

Max, who is sitting to the left of Peter, turns to look at him, flopping his dark hair off his forehead. "Hey, yeah. You've barely told us anything about it. What was it like?"

Peter reaches down, fidgets with top of the wheel on his chair, not knowing what to say. It's not like he's going to tell these guys about the nightmare, about Meena, about how the whole thing moved him in some indescribable way. Peter himself thinks the notion is weird; no doubt his friends would suspect that he'd gone completely bonkers.

"Can't really describe it," Peter says. "I don't know. It was a fire."

Doug leans forward, slamming his hands down flat on the white tabletop, nearly spilling his bowl of chicken noodle soup as he does so. His eyes are lit up, animated. "Oh, come on, man. Was it cool, like this big, crazy inferno? Was it like it is in the movies?"

"No. It wasn't *cool*," Peter responds. He glares at Doug, fed up with his idiocy. "It was a fire. The house burned down. There wasn't anything cool about it."

"Whoa. Chill, P." Doug raises his hands up in the air in surrender. He sits back in his chair, shaking his head and crossing his arms over his chest. "What's gotten into you? Did somebody, like, steal your sense of humor?"

Peter looks down at his hamburger, feeling like an ass. He knows Doug is right. He knows that a couple of months ago, he would've thought the fire was cool. He would have been psyched to share all of the gory details with his friends.

What the hell is happening to him?

"Watch out, here comes the study dork," Keith announces, breaking the tension.

Peter glances over his shoulder to see Jane rushing into the cafeteria, and he's actually happy to see her. For one, if she comes to get him now, he'll avoid having to get into describing the fire to his friends.

Jane heads straight for Peter, kinky curls flying around her face. "Hi. You ready to go to next period?"

Peter shrugs—for his friends' benefit so they don't sense that he's perfectly glad to leave with Jane at this moment. "Sure. Whatever," he says.

"Okay. Cool." Jane grabs the handlebars on the back of Peter's wheelchair, and he leans down to unlock the wheels. "Bye, guys," she says to the others.

"Bye," Max responds. Keith and Doug don't even say anything. But as Jane starts to turn Peter's chair around, as he waves good-bye to his friends, he sees that Doug is making puking motions with his hand. Peter knows that Doug and Keith will continue to mock Jane for the next couple of minutes.

But Peter is not in the mood to make fun of Jane. Because as she wheels him between the tables and toward the door, he almost feels relieved to be with her instead of Max, Keith, and Doug. Jane doesn't want anything from him. They're not friends, so she expects nothing. With his friends, Peter feels the need to be the person he was before—feels obligated to keep up a front.

With Jane he can just *be*. Because she couldn't care less.

• • •

It's four o'clock and Meena is sitting on her bed, knitting. She's had to start over since she lost the scarf she'd been working on in the fire. But she's flying along at record speed. This is where she has been for most of the day, and for a good portion of the afternoon she has been able to block out all of her thoughts and nightmares, concentrating solely on her new project, on staring at the little blue and green stitches.

But now her lower back and neck are beginning to hurt from sitting in the same position for hours, and all of her horrible feelings, all of her frightening memories, are starting to seep their way back into her brain.

The vision of that standing lamp flickering, of it sizzling and sparking, plays before Meena's mind, taunting her. Why hadn't she done anything? Why had she just sat there and watched everything burn?

Meena's throat begins to dry up, her stomach hollows out as the answer presents itself immediately. Because she enjoyed it. Sure, she was frozen with shock at first, but the longer she sat there, the more she realized that watching Steven's things burn, watching the place where it had all happened be engulfed by flames, actually gave her comfort. That was why she ultimately hadn't moved. If her parents find out that she didn't attempt to prevent the flames, that she was the one who let it get out of control . . .

But this leads Meena to an interesting realization. She stops knitting for a second, placing the needles down on her lap. If the investigators suspect that Meena was negligent, if they tell that to the Claytons and her parents, she'll never be trusted to baby-sit for Trace again. She won't be allowed. Which means she'll never have to be alone with Steven again.

This thought emboldens Meena, relaxes her just a little bit. She looks out the window, stares down at the wooden fence that divides her yard from the neighbors'. She still feels the guilt and fear, of course; these emotions have found a home deep inside Meena, but the prospect of never having to be alone with Steven again, of knowing he'll never touch her again, lightens the weight a little. Makes Meena feel like she just might be able to make it through all of this.

"Meena? Can I come in?" her mother calls from outside her door.

"Sure," Meena says. She slides down on her bed so that she's sitting on the edge.

As her mother walks in, her eyes immediately fall on Meena's scarf. "Look at that," she says. She takes a seat next to Meena and picks up the knitting, squinting at the stitches. "Very nice work."

"Thanks," Meena says. She knows her mother means it, but it isn't true. Meena's work is childlike. The scarf's just a simple pattern and her mom is capable of knitting much more elaborate things.

Her mother gently places the scarf back down. "Well," she says, folding her hands in her lap. "I just wanted to let you know that the Claytons are going to be staying with us for a while."

The floor, the entire earth, seems to drop out from under Meena. She can actually feel the color draining out of her face; she can feel the life draining out of her body. All she can do is blink. "What?"

"Sweetie," her mom responds, her brow furrowing as she looks a bit confused. "You know they won't be able to move back into their house for several weeks."

Pure fear, total rage, bubbles up inside Meena. She can't accept that this is happening. She *won't* accept it. "I thought they were staying at the Ramada," she manages to squeeze out.

Meena's mom waves the question off, shaking her head. "Your father and I wouldn't stand for it. They're our best friends. It's the least we can do."

Meena stands, though her legs feel shaky. She walks away from her mom and toward her desk, grasping the back of her swiveling chair. Her parents invited him here. No, they insisted he stay here.

"But . . . where will they sleep?" Meena asks.

Her mother shrugs. "In Noah and Micah's rooms. Steven and Lydia in one, Trace in the other. Whatever's more comfortable for them."

Meena doesn't feel like her legs can support her anymore. She slumps down into the chair and stares down at the wood floor. Noah and Micah's rooms are just down the hall. Steven is going to be staying just down the hall, only feet away from her door. . . .

"Are you all right? What's wrong?" Meena's mother asks, standing up and walking over to her.

Meena shakes her head. She can't hide her tears. Her fear. She stares down at a knot in the wood, wishing she could just disappear into it. "It's just, I don't think it's a good idea. After last night . . . I mean, I need space. I need—" Meena breaks off, knowing that she's not making any sense.

Meena's mom crosses her long, slender arms over her chest, regarding her daughter disapprovingly. "Meena. I'm surprised at you. Yes, you have been through a lot. But imagine what the Claytons have gone through. They've lost their home."

Meena grasps her thumb ring, turning it around and around. She shakes her head again. She has to make her mom understand. She can't have him living here. Under this roof. "I know," Meena says. "It's just that I really won't feel comfortable . . . at all."

"I don't understand," her mother says, her expression hardening. "I don't. I know you must be feeling confused and upset by what happened, and that's what this is all really about. And whenever you feel like it, we can talk about it." Her mother pauses for a moment, waits for Meena to say something. But Meena has no words left. She can barely breathe.

"Is our house going to feel a little crowded?" her mom continues. "Yes. Does that mean we turn our back on our friends? Absolutely not. And you know that the Claytons would do the same for us. So let's just feel lucky for what we have and be generous with it. Okay?"

No! It's not okay! Meena wants to scream. The one place she feels completely and totally safe is being ripped away from her and there's nothing she can do about it. Not even her parents will protect her. She can't respond to her mother—she can't even look at her.

Her mother lets out a heavy sigh, as if Meena is trying all of her patience. "All right. I'm sure you're just tired. Come talk to me whenever you want. In any case, they'll be moving in tomorrow." Her mother watches Meena for one more moment, apparently waiting to see if she'll say anything. When she doesn't, her mom turns and walks out of the room, closing the door behind her.

Meena lifts her head. Stares at the closed door in disbelief. Actually, she wishes it was disbelief, but she fully believes the truth she is being forced to face: her mother is on Steven's side. Both of her parents care more about Steven than they do about her. First her father forced her to go baby-sit there when she told him she wasn't feeling well and now this. Now they're welcoming him into her home. Into her haven.

And Meena has never felt more alone in her life.

CHAPTER TEN

He's here. He's *downstairs. In my house.*

Meena lies in her bed Friday, knees curled up to her chest, her head throbbing from a night of no sleep and constant crying. She hopes, she prays, that this is all just a nightmare that she will shortly wake from. But Meena knows it isn't. The details are too vivid.

The way the late morning sun is streaming through her half-open curtains, bathing the bedroom in light, the smell of the coffee brewing downstairs, the sounds of dishes clattering as her mother unloads the dishwasher, all of these things feel too real, too sharp, to be explained away by a dream. Just like Meena's pain.

She has been lying here practically motionless for a few hours. Ever since her parents came into her room this morning. She told them she couldn't, she wouldn't go to school today, and they said that was fine. She could rest. Her father went off to work and her mother stayed home to be with Meena.

And also, apparently, to welcome the Claytons.

About ten minutes ago Meena heard the front door open and close, followed by Trace's baby babble, Lydia's shrill laugh, and Steven's ugly, deep voice. Meena froze up immediately, realizing that she should have gone to school, she should have gone *anywhere* just so that she wouldn't be here, in her room, when Steven invaded her house.

Meena stares over at her desk across the room, focuses on her piles of textbooks and spiral notebooks and binders, all of the things she used to spend so much time stressing over, worrying about. What she wouldn't do to have a history exam be the worst of her problems or a swim meet the source of her greatest anxiety.

Meena clings to the soft edge of her comforter, desperation and helplessness clawing their way into her heart. Steven is downstairs, in her house, and there's nothing she can do about it. And tonight he will be footsteps away from her bedroom. From her.

Meena's stomach twists and turns. Her nerves feel like they're unraveling. This can't happen. She can't *let this* happen.

She sits up, grabbing her pillow and burying her face in it, trying to come up with some sort of plan. A way out. But Meena has run through the options countless times this morning, only to find that she has none. She could go stay at Luke or Dana's, but she basically blew them off the other day, and besides, both they and her parents would require some sort of explanation. Meena has no idea what she'd tell them.

Meena doesn't want to talk to anyone. The fear of them

knowing, of someone finding her out, still lurks within her. She just wants to be alone. And far, far away from Steven.

Meena hears the sound of Steven sneezing and she propels her pillow across the room in anger. But as she stares at the lilac pillow, she realizes there is still one possibility. An option. She could run away. Of course, Meena has no idea where she would go. And the thought that she'd be letting Steven drive her out of her own home only makes her more mad. More frustrated. But Meena allows the thought to hang there. To linger.

Meena hears footsteps coming up the stairs and her neck muscles tighten and twist with tension. She freezes, petrified. Scared that if she even moves a muscle, he'll hear her. He'll know she's listening for him. How can this be happening? How can he be allowed to take away her one safe place?

There's a light tap on the door. "Sweetie? Can I come in?"

It's her mother. Meena relaxes a bit. She stands and trudges over to her door, unlocking it, then slumps right back to her bed as her mother walks inside.

"You want to come downstairs and say hello to the Claytons?"

Meena shakes her head. "No." She has no intention of leaving this room, of venturing downstairs, as long as he is in the house.

Her mother's eyes darken. She takes another step into Meena's room, quietly closing the door behind her. "Meena, come on. We are not going to go through all of this— whatever it's about—again."

Her mother's betrayal feels like a slap in the face. It stings, igniting Meena's already raw pain. "I'm tired. I don't feel like it."

"Well, I'm sorry, but it's very rude to not at least say hello," her mother says firmly. She doesn't raise her voice, of course. Never does. But Meena knows when her mother is angry. "Your father and I will not tolerate this kind of behavior."

Meena's mother stands there, lanky arms crossed, mouth in a tightly set line, waiting. Meena knows that she's not going to budge until she agrees. She'll just keep on standing there, glaring.

Meena doesn't have it in her to fight. She knows there's no way her mom's going to let her hide out in here all day. So she decides to just get it over with. Swallow her fear, push back her terror, say hello to the bastard and have the task be behind her.

"Fine," Meena says, standing.

Her mother shakes her head as she opens the door, holding it open for Meena to walk ahead of her. "You'd think I was sending you down to the torture chamber," she says.

Meena's hands ball into fists. Her stomach somersaults. Because that's what this is. Pure torture.

She takes slow, deliberate steps down the stairs, trying to procrastinate as much as possible. Attempting to put off her pain. Her legs feel heavy, but her knees feel weak. And as Meena gets to the bottom of the stairs, as Steven's voice gets louder, as she can practically smell his presence in her house, Meena feels nothing but dread.

Just get it over with, Meena tells herself, letting out a heavy breath. *Just do it and go back upstairs.* She follows the sounds of the voices to the living room, and even though she tried to prepare herself, she is completely shocked to see the Claytons hanging out in her living room, their shopping bags filled with new clothes they've had to buy, lined up on the floor.

They're really here. They're really moving in.

Meena feels Steven's eyes on her, it makes her skin burn and itch, and she quickly focuses on Trace and Lydia, who sit on the Oriental rug on the floor, playing with some blocks.

"Hi, sweetie," Lydia says. She smiles up at Meena, but Meena can see that her eyes look tired. Drained.

"Hi," Meena says. She knows Steven is still staring at her, penetrating her, and she grabs the cuffs of her sweatshirt, fidgeting with her hands and doing her best not to look back at him.

"Mee-na!" Trace says, toddling over to her.

Meena crouches down to give Trace a kiss on the cheek as her mother sits down, grateful to have something to distract her from Steven. But she's not distracted. She's completely aware of Steven's every movement. As Meena plays with Trace's pudgy hands she sees Steven standing up out of the corner of her eye. Sees him moving away from the armchair and toward her. Meena focuses more intently on Trace, staring at his blond wisps of hair as Steven comes closer. And closer.

Trace waddles back over to his mother and Meena slowly stands, knowing that Steven is inches away from her. Finally she looks at him. She has no choice. He stands right before her.

"Well, Meen," Steven says, stuffing his hands into the pockets of his khakis. "I guess we gotta look at the bright side of this situation. At least we'll get to hang out more, right?"

Fear, panic, and hatred shoot through Meena's body, pump through Meena's veins. She wishes she could spit in Steven's face, kick him, wipe that smirk off his face. But since her mother and Lydia are there and watching, Meena simply says, "Yes," trying to muster up as much venom as she can.

She looks to her mother to signal that her duty is done, that she has been sufficiently tortured, and then she takes a step back from Steven and pointedly doesn't look his way.

"Just wanted to say hi," she tells all of them. "I'm going back to sleep now."

Meena doesn't wait for a response or for a nod of approval from her mother. She just turns and heads up the stairs, tears beginning to rise up in her.

But for once they're not just tears of guilt or of fear. They're the hot tears of anger. Just seeing Steven in her house. Seeing him making himself comfortable among her family's things. Hearing him say so casually that he's glad he'll be seeing more of her.

What more could he see? Hasn't he seen enough? Done enough to her?

And her parents! How could her parents do this to her? How can they not see how tortured she is?

No one cares about me, Meena thinks as she ducks into her room and locks the door behind her. *If they did, they'd know. If they did, they'd stop this.* She turns the radio up loud and begins to sob, burying her face in her hands.

Meena doesn't even make it to her bed. She just drops down right there on the carpet and lies down, wishing she could disappear.

• • •

Danny slumps out of the nurse's office after lunch, wanting to get as far away from the little, too bright room as possible. He was there to take his handy-dandy midday dose of pills, a chore that Danny enjoys almost as much as taking out the garbage.

Danny heads for the music wing, fidgeting with the silver chain that runs from his pocket to his belt loop as he walks. It's just so completely humiliating that the nurse has to give him his special little pills in his special little plastic cup. Like he's a mental patient or something. Danny laughs bitterly to himself. Technically, he realizes, he *is* a mental patient.

Well, whatever. Danny heads down the hallway to his right, navigating his way around a group of giggling freshmen. Danny knows that the doc is wrong about him. He doesn't have a disorder. He's not crazy. He just has lots of energy.

Not that Danny is feeling all that energetic today. In fact, he feels sort of sluggish. Flat. Totally unlike himself.

Danny is positive that this is yet another side effect of his medications. But he is not going to let the meds win out. No way. He's going to try to get his normal energy back. He knows he can if he just tries hard enough. And he's going to the perfect class to rev him up. Music theory with Mr. Vega. Danny usually cracks a million jokes in that class, and Vega is such a pushover, he hardly ever does anything to stop him.

Danny pushes open the door to the classroom, which is already filled.

"Mr. Chaiken. Nice of you to join us," Mr. Vega says, placing his hands on his hips.

Danny looks back at the teacher, this being an opportune time for a comeback. But as Danny searches his brain for one, he comes up blank. Nada. Nothing. It's like someone lifted his sense of humor or something.

At a loss, Danny just shrugs. "Sorry," he says. Then he takes the only empty seat—the one behind Jane Scott.

"Well, okay. Where were we?" Mr. Vega says, turning to the blackboard.

Danny rubs at his eyes as Mr. Vega goes on to dissect a Beethoven concerto. He sighs, bends down to pull his spiral notebook and a pen out of his backpack, and places them on the desk in front of him.

This is so pathetic. This is usually Danny's prime joke time, when he rips on everything Vega says, eliciting laughs from his classmates, being the life of the party. But right now Danny doesn't have one funny thought in his brain. Come to think of it, he doesn't have one thought. Period.

Danny stares at the back of Jane's head as Vega drones on. He zeros in on her black curls, not believing this is happening to him. He can't believe these drugs he's being forced to take are actually robbing him of his personality. They might as well just make him into a robot.

Well, Danny's still not going to give in. He flips open his notebook, turns to a blank page, and lifts his pen to commence some serious doodling. Danny is a true artiste when it comes to scribbling. His doodles are works of art. Really. Everyone at school knows that about him.

So Danny begins to draw a long, skinny line. But a moment later, when he sits back to look at the line, he frowns. He bites on the end of his pen, not knowing what he wants to do with that line. What to make of it. Frustrated, Danny turns the page. Starts again. But he soon finds himself in the same place. Totally stuck. Completely uninspired. A big zero.

Danny drops his pen. Slumps back in his seat. He doesn't believe this! He can't even draw. Not even one freakin' doodle. What the hell is going on?

"All right. These are due a week from today," Mr. Vega is saying, a stack of assignments piled in his hands.

Danny quietly, numbly watches the teacher hand out the packets, a feeling of emptiness overcoming him.

Mr. Vega steps in front of Danny's desk. Hands one of the assignments to him. The teacher smiles. Runs a hand over his semibald head. "I have to say, Mr. Chaiken, I'm impressed by your good behavior today."

Danny's face falls as the teacher walks away. A *teacher* is complimenting him on his *behavior*? In his entire life, Danny is sure that has never happened before. He knows he doesn't feel like himself, can't muster up the energy to act like himself. But when adults start noticing the difference—when the difference is big enough to comment on—there's definitely something wrong.

● ● ●

"Okay. I'll break it down for you," Josh tells Jeremy, handing him a beer-filled plastic cup. "Give you a map of the student body."

"Yeah, man. Lay it out," Jeremy says, following Josh out of the overcrowded kitchen, where everyone is vying for a space near the keg. It's Friday night and he and Josh have been at Bria's party for about half an hour now. Chris Demay, who they drove over with, basically bolted away the minute they got there, spotting a sophomore girl that he's been after for weeks. But Jeremy hasn't minded just hanging out with Josh on his own. The guy is very funny.

"Okay. So, to your left, we have the burnouts," Josh says as they walk into the huge, airy living room.

Jeremy looks over to his left, over by the stereo, to see three shaggy-haired guys and one girl, all of them with bloodshot eyes and grim expressions.

"I'd say in about twenty minutes, they'll be breaking out the whippets," Josh says.

Jeremy laughs, running a hand over his short, dark hair. He knows the type. Falls has their own version of this crew—Peter Davis, Doug Anderson, Max Kang, and Keith Kleiner.

"And over here"—Josh motions over to a long couch against a wall—"is the drama crowd. They're going to burst into a game of charades any moment now."

Jeremy nods, smiling over at the four girls with various shades of dyed hair and the two guys—one tall with a black turtleneck, sporting a junior Armani look, the other short, scrawny, and pimply. "Good call."

"What can I say?" Josh responds. "I spend way too much time with these people. Now, let's see who else we can find. . . ."

Josh heads out of the living room and down a hallway and Jeremy follows, still taking in the scene as he walks. He recognizes a number of faces from sports or just from around town, but for the most part, he's surrounded by strangers. Still, the party feels eerily familiar. Like he's in a *Twilight Zone* version of a Falls rager, and all of Jeremy's friends and classmates have simply been replaced by Kennedy clones.

"Ah. Now this is the crowd you'll probably feel most at home with," Josh announces, walking into a narrow den.

Jeremy steps inside the room, which is dark except for the flickering light of the big-screen TV and is filled with some guys that he recognizes from football.

Josh looks to the screen, then rolls his eyes. "No comment needed," he whispers, so as not to disturb the guys from concentrating on whatever it is they're watching.

"That's it, baby! Come on!" Steve Corelli, the quarterback, yells out.

A couple of the other guys hoot and holler and Jeremy looks to the TV to see what they're screaming about. And the minute he does, he can't help but mimic Josh and roll his eyes as well. They're watching porn. And Jeremy has no problem with that, he really doesn't. But why would you want to watch one of these flicks during a party, when all the girls you know are in the next room? It just seems . . . wrong.

"This might be my crowd, but this is not my scene, man," Jeremy whispers to Josh. On the screen a second woman joins a couple that is already in the process of making out. Uncomfortable, Jeremy quickly averts his eyes, taking a quick sip of beer.

Josh gives Jeremy a sideways smile, his brown eyes crinkling in the corners. "Didn't think it was."

A couple of the guys turn their attention away from the TV at the sound of Josh's voice. One of them—Zach Chernak, a linebacker—raises his eyebrows. He tosses a Dorito at Josh but misses, hitting the wall behind him instead.

"Hey, Strauss!" Zach calls. "Sorry we didn't round up any fag porn for you to jerk off to!"

A few of the guys laugh and Jeremy feels a surge of anger tensing his neck, his hands. He wants to strangle Zach's thick neck. But Josh calmly stands there, a big smile plastered on his face.

"No worries, Chernak," Josh retorts. "Unlike you, I

don't need to depend on video—or myself—for sex. But go ahead. Enjoy the fantasy while you can."

"Whoo! Good one, Strauss!" one of the guys screams out. A bunch of the other guys burst out in laughter—including Jeremy. He is so impressed by the swift and cool way that Josh fired out that comeback. It was truly masterful.

Zach, however, is not smiling. He gets up from the brown leather armchair he's sitting in, as if he's going to walk right over and start a fight with Josh. Jeremy takes a step forward, getting ready to protect his friend if need be. But then Steve Corelli hollers, "Check out those tits!" and all of the guys' attention—including Zach's—returns to the TV.

Josh turns to Jeremy. "I've had enough. You?"

Jeremy nods. "Plenty, dude."

Josh heads out of the den and Jeremy follows, walking with Josh down the hallway until they reach a door. Josh opens it and they walk through it, finding themselves outside by the garage. Two guys and a girl are playing basketball in the driveway, but aside from them, no one else is out here.

Probably because it's kind of cold. Jeremy places his beer down on one of the concrete steps so that he can zip up his leather jacket.

Josh sits down on one of the steps. He looks up at Jeremy. "Mind if we chill out here for a sec? I need some air."

"Whatever. No problem," Jeremy says. As he drops down next to Josh, he realizes that he has no need to be partying inside. He's having a good time just hanging out with Josh. The guy is so smart . . . and funny . . . and the way he handled that idiot in there. . . .

Jeremy glances at Josh now. He seems to be very contemplative, his dark brown eyes intensely focused on the middle distance, his mouth firmly set. Jeremy frowns, wondering if Josh is bummed out by what happened. It has to be so hard. Jeremy has tried to figure out many times—too many, probably—how Josh deals.

Jeremy clears his throat. "You okay?"

Josh looks to Jeremy, snapping out of his trance. "Huh? Oh, you mean Chernak?" Josh shrugs, takes a sip of his beer. "No big deal. I'm used to it."

Jeremy stares at Josh, amazed. Josh's casual tone, the way he said the words, make it seem like he actually means them. Like it *is* no big deal. But how can that be true?

Jeremy scratches at the back of his neck. Fidgets with his gold pendant. "You're saying that it doesn't get to you?"

Josh gives Jeremy one of his lopsided smiles. A smile that brings a calmness, a gentleness to his entire face. "Sure, it gets to me. A little. But it's nothing like it was when I first came out."

Jeremy looks down to the ground, at his brown loafers, flushing a bit. *When I first came out.* Of course, Jeremy knows that Josh is out of the closet, he's even thought about what it must have been like for him to come out, but something about hearing Josh actually say it out loud unnerves Jeremy. Scares him.

Jeremy picks up his plastic cup. The fact that Josh is

185

out of the closet does also impress Jeremy, though. It impresses him that the guy can be so brave.

Jeremy swallows. "What was it like?" He doesn't take his eyes off the beer. He stares down fixedly at the thin layer of foam. "I mean, when you came out?"

"Honestly?" Josh laughs. "It sucked."

Jeremy lifts his head and looks back at Josh, feeling a sense of relief that he can't explain or describe. "Really?"

"Oh yeah." Josh places his arms behind him, leaning back on the palms of his hands. "Got into many fights. With my parents. My friends. Random people at school. You definitely learn who your true friends are."

Jeremy nods, an image of Mike Chumsky in angry mode popping into his brain. Jeremy can only imagine what Mike's reaction would be to someone coming out of the closet. "I'd think so."

"Yeah," Josh says. "But you know what? It was totally, one hundred percent worth it."

That relief that Jeremy was feeling a moment ago takes a sudden downturn, transforming into anxiety. His heartbeat feels a little too rapid, his mouth, a little too dry. "Really?"

"Definitely." Josh sits back up, resting his elbows on his knees. For some reason, Jeremy finds himself noticing that Josh has very long eyelashes. Jeremy shifts as he sits, not happy with the direction this all seems to be going in.

"To be able to be true to myself? Live how I want to live? Go out with who I want to go out with?" Josh says. "Can't beat that."

Jeremy wishes he could just walk away. Just walk away and end this conversation, never to have one like it again. But he can't stop himself from staring back at Josh, from being totally intrigued by what he's saying, from noticing the way Josh's brown V-necked sweater matches his eyes. . . .

"There is one thing that's especially crappy about being gay in high school, though," Josh says.

Jeremy raises his eyebrows. He needs to hear this. He *wants* to hear this. "What's that?"

Josh runs a hand through his blondish red hair. "Dating. There aren't a whole lot of gay teens walking around. And then if you do meet one, he's not necessarily someone you're into. Someone you're attracted to. Know what I mean?"

Jeremy's heart is racing. He feels his palms sweating against the plastic cup and he places the beer down, rubbing his hands against his khaki cargo pants. "I guess," he says, his voice sounding unsteady. Unsure.

Josh nods. Takes another sip of beer, watching Jeremy carefully. "It's kind of like, if you do meet someone, you just gotta go for it."

Jeremy swallows. Josh is looking at him so intensely, so focused. Those big brown eyes of his seem to be asking Jeremy a question—a question that Jeremy's not sure he can answer.

• • •

Frantic, crazed, and scared out of her mind, Meena pulls her blue duffel bag out from under her bed that night and unzips it, opening it up. She can't go on like

187

this. She can't live here, in this house, with Steven always nearby. Lurking. Threatening.

Meena rubs at the tears that are perpetually in her eyes, then rushes over to her dresser, opening the top drawer and grabbing some socks and underwear. The one lucky thing about today was that Steven had left around noon to go teach a class at Skidmore, so Meena had at least felt safe enough to come down to the kitchen for lunch. But other than that, she's been holed up here in her room. Forced to hear the sounds of him talking, laughing, walking all throughout her house while she hid in her bedroom, her door securely locked. She refused to come down for dinner and neither one of her parents has asked her what's wrong. It's obvious that they're just angry and disappointed that Meena's being *rude* to their guests. They can't even get past that long enough to care about her. When she told her mom she wasn't going to eat, she just looked at Meena like she was nuts.

Which, at this point, she probably is. Steven has officially made her crazy. And living under the same roof with him will only drive Meena over the edge. He always haunts her thoughts, her dreams, but to have him right here, right in front of her face? Where she can feel him watching her at all times? Where he's close enough that she can smell his aftershave—the same stuff he was wearing that night?

No way. Meena can't take it.

Meena tosses the socks and underwear into her bag, then tries to clear her head to think of what else she might need. Toothbrush. Toothpaste. Deodorant. Brush. The bare necessities. But in the state that Meena's in, the only thing that truly seems necessary is to get away from Steven. To remove herself from this unbearable situation. Still, Meena hurries into her bathroom to gather the toiletries. And as she does so, she wonders where the hell she's going to go. She has absolutely no idea.

As Meena throws all of the bathroom items into her bag, she thinks of those after-school specials she used to watch on ABC. Teenage runaway. Abused girl. Good girl gone bad. Her head pounds. She can't believe this is what her life has become. That this has happened to her. *Steven* has happened to her.

Shaking, Meena grabs her sneakers. Stuffs her feet into them. Just as she's lacing the shoes up, she hears peals of laughter coming from downstairs. Not just one person laughing—all of them. Her mom. Her dad. Lydia. Steven.

Meena bolts up. The sound of the four adults being happy, enjoying themselves, suddenly makes Meena very, very angry. Steven then says something in a loud, half-laughing voice, and the other three burst out again.

Meena feels like punching someone. Like throwing something out the window. She wants to punish them all for laughing while she's up here ready to poke her eyes out. And she's so unbelievably mad. Mad at her parents for being so oblivious, mad at Lydia for not knowing that her husband is a complete scumbag, and mad at Steven for being the scumbag that he is.

Meena kicks at her duffel bag, sending it flying to the

opposite corner of the room.

And of course, she's mad at herself for letting this all happen. For being such a horrible person.

Meena walks over to her duffel bag. Scoops it up. And right then and there, an idea forms in her head. She shoulders the bag, thinking the idea through. Yes. This is the answer. The way. The *only* way.

She walks to her door but hesitates for a moment when the sounds of Aretha Franklin come wafting upstairs. Her mother's favorite album.

If Meena goes through with this, she won't just be punishing herself. She'll be punishing them. Her parents. At that moment she hears the sound of Steven's voice again and her mind is quickly made up. She unlocks the door.

Meena is going to do something. Right now.

CHAPTER ELEVEN

As Jeremy stares back at Josh, all of the details of this moment seem magnified. Intensified. The rhythmic sound of the basketball bouncing in the distance. The bright outdoor light shining directly behind Josh. The slight woodsy scent of Josh's aftershave . . .

Josh's aftershave? What the hell is he doing noticing another guy's aftershave? Jeremy quickly looks away from Josh, his toned shoulders tensing up.

"Jeremy? You get what I'm saying?" Josh asks gently.

Jeremy looks back up. Finds himself staring at the silver cuff bracelet that Josh wears on his wrist, unable to meet his gaze.

"Yes. I think I do," Jeremy says. He means for his words to come out harshly, for his tone to be sharp edged, but they come out sounding gentle and soft instead.

Josh nods and smiles that incredible smile. And then he looks at Jeremy that way. That way that implies that he wants to kiss him.

Jeremy's body wages a war with itself. His stomach

drops with anxiety, with horror, telling him to just run away, bolt as fast as he can, while his heart rises up into his skull, pounding in his ears, telling him what he wants. What he really wants.

Maybe I could kiss Josh. Just to see what it's like, Jeremy thinks, his heart winning out over his stomach. After all, no one has to know.

Josh begins to lean in toward Jeremy, coming closer. . . .

A slide show of Jeremy's perfect life presents itself in his brain: his beautiful girlfriend, his popular status, his loving parents. . . .

Jeremy quickly stands before Josh can come any closer. *I can't. I can't do this,* Jeremy thinks, taking a step away from Josh and knocking over his beer in the process. "Let's go back inside," Jeremy says, cracking his knuckles and shifting his weight from one foot to the other. "It's getting cold."

Jeremy sees the look of shock, of disappointment, register on Josh's face, and his heart twists. He quickly turns and opens the door that leads inside, stepping into the hall before Josh can say anything.

"Jeremy. Wait," Josh calls, coming up behind Jeremy. "I'm sorry if I upset you. Can we talk for a sec?"

Jeremy stops. Turns around to look at Josh. Which is a big mistake. Because he's standing so close to him that he can't help himself from staring into his eyes. From wanting to kiss him more than anything in the world.

Josh touches Jeremy's hand—lightly—but it sends the

most powerful feelings of attraction, of desire, soaring through Jeremy's body. This one movement does more for Jeremy than any of Tara's kisses ever have. It's all of his worst fears, confirmed in one touch.

Jeremy just stands there stupidly, his heart slamming against his chest, his stomach tied up in knots, that inner battle still tearing him apart.

"Come on. We can talk in here," Josh says, tipping his head to motion to a small, dark room that looks like an office.

Jeremy follows Josh inside, knowing that they're not going to talk. And the really scary part is, that's okay with him. More than okay.

Josh turns around. Grabs Jeremy's hand again, more firmly this time. Josh's eyes lock with Jeremy's. His pulse races to warp speed.

Anticipation, excitement overtake Jeremy's body, beating down those feelings of fear and anxiety. And this time, as Josh leans in closer . . . and closer, Jeremy doesn't move away.

He allows Josh's lips to meet his, allows the kiss to happen, and man, is he glad he does. He feels like he's just waking up from a very long slumber, the kiss sending tingles from the top of his head to his toes. Josh lifts a hand, massages the back of Jeremy's neck, and Jeremy feels his arms and legs weaken with pleasure at his touch.

Jeremy has never, ever felt anything like this before.

• • •

It's ten o'clock Friday night, and Peter lies in bed, not doing anything. Not playing Sega, not watching TV, not reading a magazine. He just lies there, staring up at the round light fixture on the stucco ceiling, wondering how many damn bugs have gotten caught in that light, how many flies have flown in there and fried to an early death.

Death. Peter squints up at the light. *One, two, three, four, five . . .* Peter can count at least five little black lumps. Five dead flies.

"Whoo-hoo!"

Peter turns his head toward his open window as he hears a guy drunkenly yell out the exclamation, followed by a blast of Kid Rock and the grating roar of a car's engine. The blur of noise passes just as quickly as it arrived. No doubt it was some jerk standing in a convertible, trying too hard to show the world what a good time he's having. Still, it makes Peter realize how lame he is, cooped up in his room on a Friday night, doing absolutely nothing.

Peter sits up, leans his back up against the wall. He can hear the muffled sounds coming from the TV in the living room and he wonders if this is what his life has truly come to. Staying home with the 'rents, doing nothing.

No. It can't be. Peter looks down at his lifeless legs. He grabs his pillow, holding it with a tight, angry grasp. He can't let his legs defeat him. He can't just lie in his bed for the rest of his life. It will kill him, destroy his brain cells one by one.

Peter doesn't want to die. He sometimes thinks he does, thinks he'd be better off if he just ended his suffering once and for all, if he just accepted his punishment and was done with it, but those are just thoughts. Not reality.

Peter wants to live. But not like this. Not paralyzed. Not stuck in a wheelchair, dependent on others for the rest of his life, never driving again, never running. Never walking. Hasn't he been punished enough? He's learned his lesson. The guilt is still there. Has been since he was ten. Always will be. Sometimes it's so strong, it's paralyzing in and of itself. Why does he have to be physically paralyzed, too?

Peter swallows and, for the first time since the accident, he thinks about trying to move his legs. About trying to fight. Not give in.

Peter takes in a deep breath. Closes his eyes. Concentrates. Squeezes his hands on the flat, foam-filled pillow.

He doesn't even know where to begin. After all, how do you try to do something you never had to think about before? Something that was just completely natural? But Peter tries just the same. He focuses on his leg muscles, his feet muscles. His toes. He visualizes them, tells his brain to move them. Even just a little bit. Just a centimeter, a millimeter.

Peter's brain doesn't listen, though. His legs don't budge. His toes don't wiggle. Peter scrunches his eyes shut tighter. He grimaces, strengthening his grip on the pillow, breathing in deep and focusing all of his energy, all of his working, alert muscles on moving his legs.

Peter can feel his face heating up, he can feel the sweat pouring down his forehead, but he keeps trying. *Move,* he thinks, clenching his jaw so tight, his mouth begins to ache. *Move. I don't care how much. Just move!*

Peter's arm and neck muscles start to feel strained, tired. His body is soaked with sweat, his gray T-shirt is drenched. Sticky. Peter lets out a grunt of exhaustion. Of defeat.

He opens his eyes, only to look at his motionless legs—those two useless, pathetic slabs of flesh. Frustrated, angry, Peter begins to hit his legs with his pillow. Hard. He keeps hitting them and hitting them until tears spring to his eyes from the exertion, until all his energy is sapped. Then he collapses flat on the bed, humiliated and mad.

That freaky dream of his—the one where everyone's asking for his help—pops into his brain and Peter lets out a short, bitter laugh. Right. Like he's supposed to help Meena, or anyone for that matter? He can't even help himself.

He's pathetic. Weak. A loser.

Peter now shakes a little bit, he shudders, and his cheeks are wet with tears he didn't even know he was shedding. He tastes the saltiness as the tears reach his mouth, feels the utter despair as he swallows them down.

Peter knows it's his fault he's like this. He committed an unspeakable atrocity. Yes, it was years ago, but he knew that one day it would catch up with him. Knew it with every fiber of his being. And now he's been sentenced for life. Imprisoned. Paralyzed.

He can't stand to keep his eyes open any longer because when he does, all he sees are his legs. Legs that might as well be cut off and removed rather than dragged around. Peter closes his eyes, hoping to escape his depression, his suffering, if only for a couple of hours.

But the minute Peter's eyes are shut, all of his terrors, all of his horrible memories, come barreling toward him. *The blaring headlights crashing into the car door. The sight of the bright red blood spilling down his face. The realization that he couldn't feel a thing below his waist. The looks of horror, of panic, staring down at him. The sirens. The stretcher. His pounding head, his aching, torn body. The gun. The gun in his hands.*

Peter's eyes fly open. He sits up. The tears rush down his face, the chills run up and down his arms. He can't take this anymore. He can't be tortured this way. Moments ago he thought that he wanted to live, but what's the point? How can anyone live like this? With all this guilt, all this pain, all these awful, hideous memories haunting him whenever he closes his eyes?

Peter grabs his digital alarm clock off his nightstand and yanks on it, ripping its cord out of the socket. He throws the clock across the room, uses all of his anger to propel it, causing it to smash against the opposite wall. The clock's plastic face shatters to pieces.

What the hell is he supposed to do?

Peter drops his head. He stares down at his blue comforter. He can't live like this. He can't. Not when there's nothing to balance out the pain. No one who really cares. Not one single thing to be happy about.

Maybe he should just do it. Just get the gun. Finish himself off. He probably should have done it ages ago.

Then, as if someone has draped a heating pad over his shoulders, Peter feels himself start to grow warm. It spreads from his shoulders up his neck, into his face, finally causing his wet scalp to tingle. Then it makes its way down his chest, through his stomach, along his arms, down to his waist, where it would go on to warm his legs if he could feel them.

At first Peter thinks he must be getting a fever, but it can't be. It isn't the frantic heat of a fever.

This warmth is pleasant. Protective. Lulling. Like when he was a little boy and would fall asleep in front of the TV and his father would wrap a fleece blanket around him like a cocoon and carry him to bed.

Peter's shoulders slowly relax. He has no idea what this is, where it comes from—he has never felt this sensation before. Still, he lies all the way down, welcoming the feeling, allowing it to comfort him.

He doesn't question. Doesn't wonder. He just accepts, grateful that all of a sudden, out of nowhere, he feels tranquil. Peaceful. And calm.

Every muscle, every nerve cell, seems like it's melting as Peter relaxes. He smiles. Closes his eyes. And he realizes that there's one more thing he's feeling, something he hasn't felt in months. Years.

As Peter drifts off into sleep, he feels full of hope.

• • •

Meena hesitates once more before opening her door. Does she really want to do this? Does she really want to punish all of them? Including herself?

Meena's grip loosens on the glass doorknob. Her palm

198

sweats. The thought of going down there and saying what she has to say terrifies her. But what choice does she have? She has to do something so that she'll never be trusted to be around the Claytons again. Something to stop her from having to live in the same house as him. Something to break her out of this hell.

She has to escape.

Confused, torn, and drained, Meena lets out a shaky breath, trying to collect herself as best she can. But when she attempts to gain some clarity by closing her eyes, she's immediately invaded by an image of Steven leaning in toward her. Kissing her. Touching her. Meena's heartbeat quickens. She can smell the liquor on his breath, feel the roughness of his skin.

Meena's eyes fly open and she swings open her bedroom door. By going through with her idea, she may cause him a little suffering in return—show him that maybe, just maybe, she's not the only one to blame.

Meena grips the worn strap of her duffel as she stalks to the stairs. She hesitates once again before walking down them, stopping to listen in on their conversation.

"We've barely seen her since we moved in," Steven is saying. "Is she okay?"

"Yes, we're sorry about that," Meena's father says. "I think she's still just shaken up about the fire. . . ."

"She'll be fine," Meena's mother says. "She's just a child, Steven. It'll take some time, but she'll bounce back."

Meena freezes up. She can't believe they're talking

about her. That they're sitting there, discussing her feelings and her behavior with Steven. Talking about her like she's "just a child." And she can imagine Steven's face. All concern. All sympathy for her parents. How can he sit there and pretend to be their friend when he knows what he and Meena have done?

Meena swallows, trying to gulp down the guilt, the self-blame, so that she can bury it and be rid of it once and for all. But it's no use. The guilt is always there, always controlling her. And so she begins to slowly, carefully walk down the stairs, knowing this is the only solution. The only way to punish all of them, including herself, including her mother and father, in one fell swoop. This will make her clueless parents open their eyes. Force them to see what a horrible daughter they have. To finally realize how blind they've been.

Meena reaches the living room and she pauses in the doorway. She waits for all of them to stop talking. To notice her standing there. Her mother and Lydia are sitting on the couch, her father on the armchair. Steven is sprawled out on the floral lounge chair, a glass of brandy or some sort of after-dinner drink in his hand.

Her father is the first to see her. "Meen!" He smiles, his brown eyes lighting up. "Decided to join us?"

They all turn to look at her now. She sees her mother notice the duffel bag, her eyebrows scrunching together, a question forming on her lips.

So Meena speaks up before any of them can say

anything more. She takes a second to look right at each of their faces—even Steven's. In fact, she allows her eyes to linger on him. She wants to see his reaction.

Her stomach feels queasy and her limbs start to weaken, so she spits the words out as quickly as possible. "I did it," she says. "It was me. I started the fire."

Meena stands there for only a millisecond longer, just long enough to see the shock register in his light eyes. Then she turns and runs out, slamming the door behind her.